The Bench

I0531442

THERESA SEDERHOLT

The Bench
Copyright© 2016 by Theresa Sederholt

The author acknowledges the copyrighted or trademarked status and trademark owners of the following wordmarks mentions in this work of fiction: The United States Coast Guard. The United States Air Force. The Veteran's Administration. Skype. The Freedom Tower. 911 Memorial. Shake Shack. The Department of Veteran's affairs. Bank of America. Starbucks. Eric Church "Three Year Old." Cole Swindell "You Should Be Here." Maxwell Air Force Base. Walter Reed hospital. Ikea. Charlie Brown. Abita draft root beer.

This is a work of fiction. Names, characters, businesses, places, events, and incidents are either the products of the author's imagination or used in a fictitious manner. Any resemblance to actual persons, living or dead, or actual events is purely coincidental.

This book contains strong language and deals with mental health issues. It is not intended for anyone under the age of 18.

Publisher: Theresa Sederholt ©
Cover designer: Robin Harper, Wicked By Design.
Editor: Jacquelyn Ayres.
Formatter: Stacey Blake, Champagne Formats.

Proceeds from this book go to The Gary Sinise Foundation. You can find out more about them at:
www.garysinisefoundation.org

ISBN: 978-0-9976692-3-7

Thank you every one who has served our country. It's because of you that we have the liberties we enjoy everyday. I would like to give a special shout out to Jonathan Gunther, Technical Sergeant E-6.

PTSD affects so many people. Not everyone fits into the same box. What works for some might not work for others. If you would like to find out more about Mick's treatment, please visit the U.S. Department of Veteran's Affairs at:

www.ptsd.va.gov/public/treatment/therapy-med/treatment-ptsd.asp

You can find out more about Mick Callan, in The Unraveled Trilogy.
The Unraveling of Raven
Darkness into Dawn
Shattered Lies

Chapter One

Mick

Everywhere I go, I hear the cries of the people. Little kids begging for help—help from me. There is no language barrier when it comes to fear and pain. No matter where I am, I can't break away from the sounds in my head of twisting metal. The smell of burning jet fuel is embedded into my brain.

Going back to Nebraska has never been an option. It hasn't been my home for years. I can never go back to Covington; too many memories. My aunt and uncle have since passed. Everyone else has moved on without me. Hell, life has moved on without me. New York City is my last hope. Maybe seeing where the towers once stood will help me remember why I went, why so many of my friends only came back somewhat alive? This isn't living life; this is nothing more than existing.

The bus ride from Bethesda is long. I fight the urge to close my eyes. I know if I do, the nightmares will come. I don't trust myself in confined spaces. I don't know if I ever will again.

The construction on the Freedom tower is already underway. The renderings of the buildings show that it will be bigger than the original towers. It's huge; it's America's way of telling the terrorist to fuck off. I walk by the 911 Memorial at least a dozen times, but I can't bring myself to go in. I shake my head in disgust, give up, and try to find the Department of Veteran's Affairs. I need to let them know where I am. The line is out the door, but it's not like I have anything better to do. When I finally get to the front desk, the information clerk hands me a form to fill out and then it's *wait* . . . all over again. They want a New York address. Damn it, I don't have one, and I'm not even sure I want one. The one thing I know, for sure, is that the only postal address for Hell is what's inside my head right now. When my number is finally called, I explain to the administrative assistant that I just got into town. She suggests I go to a mailbox place, get a box and then come back again. It's a start; something is better than nothing. Before I leave, she assures me the postal places are everywhere. I duck into the nearest one and show the clerk my driver's license with my old Louisiana address. She issues me a box and puts in the change of address form. At least now I have something to show the Department of Veteran's Affairs.

I walk down the city streets, trying to take it all in.

Maybe this wasn't such a good idea? Cars gridlocked and their horns blaring. There are so many people rushing to get nowhere fast. There's an underground subway system that I know I can't go anywhere near. There is a smell coming out of the grates along with the screeching of the train. It sounds like twisted metal, a trigger for me. This city is filled with so many homeless people, everyone with a story to be told. Some of them are veterans who could really use the services more than me. If I could get out of my own head, I wouldn't need anyone. I find a Bank of America, withdraw some cash out of my account and then put in a change of address. After that, I finally find a nice bench in the warm, afternoon sunshine. My hands are filled with, at least, a dozen pamphlets of services available. Unfortunately, the wait for help is more than I can handle. Most guys I know can't wait that long. If they are reaching out for help, they are at the end, hanging on to that last straw, trying to claw their way to the top of that murky water.

Day turns into night and starts all over again. It's true what they say: this city never really sleeps. There is a Starbucks across the street from my bench. I head over and order some overpriced stuff and use the restroom. I decide to leave the pamphlets in the john; maybe someone can find what they are looking for. I head out, get my food, and head back to my bench, my home for the unforeseeable future.

One day leads to another and after a while, I lose count. The manager of Starbucks lets me come in, before he closes, so I can wash up. There is kindness here; you only have to open your eyes to see it.

I fight every night to suppress my nightmares. Some nights are worse than others. I've officially declared the bench my home. It's crazy that I'm becoming so protective of it, worrying that, when I'm gone, someone might take it from me. Still, I've been venturing out a little bit further from my bench every day. Even though I have no place to be, I'm somewhere—anywhere—just not inside my own head.

I found a church that has a soup kitchen. After speaking to the pastor, he allows me to volunteer. It's only one day a week, but it's something I can do—no questions or long conversations—just serve hungry people. Today, I'm dishing out chili and that's when I notice her. She looks familiar. I realize I've seen her at the Starbucks across the street from my bench. It's such a big city, yet, such a small world. She talks to each person she's giving food to, not making them embarrassed because of their situation.

"Hey, mister, are you going to dish that out or what?"

"Yes, I'm sorry." I go back to my job and by the time the last person is through the line, she's gone.

"Excuse me, Pastor John, who was the girl on salad today?"

"Another one of God's angels. Can you stay and help with clean up?"

"Sure, back to reality, sir. When I'm done, would you mind if I showered before I leave?"

"Of course not. Would you like me to see if I can get you a bed in one of the shelters?"

"No thank you. Save it for someone who really needs

it." I know he means well, but I don't trust myself to sleep in a room with others. What if the nightmares come? What if I can't control them? What if I hurt someone? It's best I head back to my bench. It's safe and, for now, that's enough.

Chapter Two

The sunshine is brighter than usual or maybe I'm just a little bit more tired than usual. Sleeping on this bench doesn't do my broken body any good. The only thing it helps is my damaged mind.

"Excuse me, sir, would you mind if I sit here?"

I look up and it's her. "Sure, have a seat." I slide over, giving her plenty of room. She passes me a cup of coffee and a bag from Starbucks.

"Thank you. You didn't have to. Please, let me pay you." I reach into my pocket for cash. She holds up her hand to stop me.

"No, really, it's my treat. I noticed you yesterday at the church; you had the chili station and I was on the salad station. I had to leave early."

"Yes, I just started volunteering at the church."

"Are you new in town?"

"What gave it away?"

"No accent, for starters." She smiles and, for some reason, it's comforting.

"My name is, Mick—Mick Callan. I'm originally from Nebraska. I just got out of the Air Force."

"Why New York?"

"A friend of mine talked about New York City all the time, so I figured why not. What about you, where are you from?" I smile and tilt my coffee cup towards her. "No accent."

"I'm originally from D.C., but New York is now my home. I teach second grade at Weinstein Academy, a private school not far from here. Do you know what you want to do now that you're out of the Air Force?"

"Right now I'm just taking one day at a time, trying to figure out where I fit in, you know . . . in the grand scheme of things."

She looks at her watch and I don't know why but I don't want this to end. "Well, Mick, I need to get to work."

She gets up to leave and I realize I don't know her name. "Miss, wait! I don't even know your name."

She turns and she's got the biggest, brightest smile I think I've ever seen. "It's a mystery, have a good day, Mick."

She turns and runs off. "Thanks again for the breakfast," I call after her. And just like that, she's gone. When I look through the bag, I find water, a protein bar, a bag of nuts, and a sandwich. I stash everything but the sandwich in my backpack. I quickly eat it and head out for the day.

Today I decide to head to Central Park. I heard it's peaceful and I really want to see the Strawberry Fields living memorial to John Lennon. He was one of music's greatest storytellers, who died such a tragic death. Why is it so hard for everyone to get along? I spent years fighting for peace, isn't that the ultimate oxymoron.

It's a long walk, but that's okay, I've got no place else to be. The park is better than I thought possible. There are so many people going about their business. I head over to Strawberry Fields and I can't help but think John Lennon would be proud. People are sitting around singing, but the best part are the kids playing together without a care in the world. If only the whole world could be seen the way children see it. No race or religion, just kids being kids.

Another morning, another fitful night on my bench. Yeah, somehow this bench has become permanently mine. This time I'm up early, looking for her. I check my watch, maybe I missed her or maybe she's not coming today. I'm about to give up and go get some coffee when I see her round the corner and head into Starbucks. When she comes out she quickly crosses the street and heads toward me.

"Good morning, Mick. I have something for you." She puts down our coffees and hands me a bright-pink rubber mat.

"Okay, I'll bite; what's this for?"

"It's a yoga mat. Sorry that it's pink, but it's my spare. I figured if you're going to sleep on this bench, you could use this as a cushion. I mean those bars must be killing your back."

She's very nonchalant about my situation. "How do you know I sleep here all night long?" I ask.

She cocks her head to the side and opens her eyes wide. For the first time, I notice they are a beautiful shade of violet. "I was not born yesterday. I'm not judging you, but apparently you don't want to go to a shelter, so at least use the mat."

"Sounds like you're in teacher mode to me."

"Very funny; more like friend mode."

"When I was at Central Park yesterday, I noticed there was a sign for free yoga classes. I could use it at the class. Are you ready to tell me your name?"

"Running late today. See you tomorrow, Mick."

She's gone and I'm left holding a pink yoga mat. When I unroll it, I see the initials R.A. Well, at least that's a start. I grab my coffee and hurry to the park. I get there just as the class is starting. I'm not new to yoga, so at least I know how to do it. Unfortunately, my battered body is fighting me on every pose. The instructor ends the class with fifteen minutes of meditation. My doctors at Bethesda suggested meditation every time I felt the panic begin to rise. I close my eyes and really try. The sound of crunching metal, the smell of jet fuel, the heat of the fire . . . burning my skin.

"Excuse me, sir, are you okay?"

My eyes fly open at her touch. My fists are filled with dirt and grass. I'm finding it difficult to breathe. I focus on her face, slowing down my breathing, coming back to reality. "Sorry, I'm fine. Thank you." I quickly get up, roll up my mat, and leave. I probably scared that poor woman half to death. I might not be going back there anytime soon.

I need a shower and a hot meal. I don't want to take advantage of Pastor John's kindness. I heard some of the people at the church talking about a big mission in the Bowery. No time like the present to give it a try. When I finally get there, I stand across the street and look at the large red door. Apparently, it's the door that most people are familiar with. So here I stand, with my backpack and my new pink yoga mat, afraid to take that step.

"You know the first step is the hardest."

I don't answer him; I know he's there. Dominic was my wingman. He's always in my head, just out of arms reach. The last person I pulled from the wreck, the one I couldn't save.

"Take the step, Mick. Don't be a sorry ass."

I walk across the street, mumbling that I'm not a sorry ass, as if he could hear me. When I step inside, I'm blown away. They offer so much and expect nothing. Showers, clean clothes, classes, food, and shelter. I start with a shower, clean clothes, and food. When I'm done, I head into the sanctuary. I've always been a spiritual man, even when I thought my God wasn't listening, even when I sometimes lose my way. I always seem to find my way back . . . somehow. When the service is over, I hang behind; I want to thank the pastor.

"Sir, thank you for all the help you offer here."

"You're welcome. I'm Pastor Clarence. Will you be staying tonight?"

"No, thank you. I would, however, like to make a donation."

"If you're in need, then maybe you should use it toward getting on your feet."

I press the cash into his hand. "This helps me more than I can explain." I leave him there staring at the cash in his hands. I head back to my bench, my home.

Chapter Three

It's Saturday morning, and I don't expect to see her today. The mat is a blessing on this hard bench. I try stretching my body out a little bit at a time but some days nothing wants to move.

"Mick, are you going to sleep the day away?"

When I open my eyes, she's standing there with a bag of food in her hands. "I didn't think I would see you today." I quickly get up and roll up the mat.

"How did the mat work for you?"

"Great. No one even commented on the color; thank you. So, R, do you live around here?"

"Trying to figure out my name? Nope, I don't live near here, but my work is not too far away, which is why I'm always here during the week. Today, however, I came here to spend some time with you."

"Why?"

"Honestly, I'm not sure. Something was telling me I should, so here I am."

"Are you going to tell me about yourself?" I prod. She's smiling and when she does, her eyes seem brighter.

"Maybe a little. Other than my name, what do you want to know?"

"You're a tough cookie. Do you always talk to strangers?"

"You're not a stranger; we have coffee together every day."

I laugh and it's the first time in a long time that I feel I can. "Have you always wanted to live in New York City?"

"No. I moved here for my job, but I love it here. Did you always live in Nebraska?"

"I was born there but when I was thirteen, my parents died in a car accident. I went to live with my aunt and uncle in a small town down south called Covington Louisiana. I went to college there and thought I would grow old there."

"Why did you leave?"

"I always knew I would serve my country, but when 911 happened, it just made my conviction even stronger."

"Exactly how long have you been out of the Air Force?"

"I've been back for six months," I answer. She doesn't say anything, just sipping her coffee in silence. "All of the sudden, you got very quiet . . . are you okay?"

Her smile is gone and she has a solemn look on her face. "Yes, I don't want to press you for answers you might not want to give me, so I'm waiting for you to tell me whatever you want me to know, on your terms."

"You're easy to talk to, R."

"Well, I try to listen with an open heart and an open

mind. Everyone has a story to tell, it's just a matter of taking the time to really listen."

"I was hurt in Iraq and sent stateside. I have nightmares, bad ones. I was diagnosed with PTSD I'm not good yet in a confined space, so I sleep here." I wave my hand around the open space as if I'm showing her a beautiful uptown apartment and not a dirty old park bench.

"Have you looked into some of the services available to you?"

"Yeah, before I left Bethesda, the doctors gave me drugs, which I don't like taking. They also gave me a bunch of pamphlets about starting over and dealing with PTSD It's hard to talk to anyone about it, let alone to a total stranger."

"I'm a stranger?"

"We've had coffee together every day; were not strangers." We both laugh and I find I'm relaxing a little bit more. I turn the tables on her. "Your turn; tell me something."

"I'm adopted. When I was fifteen, my adopted mom died of breast cancer. My dad . . . well, let's just say I couldn't stay there anymore. I ran away and eventually made it through high school and then college. I took the job that I'm doing now and I never looked back."

"You're a brave lady."

"Not really; I'm a survivor. I don't know any other way."

"Have you ever been in love? I mean, you're a beautiful woman and I would think men would be knocking down your door." She hesitates and now I'm second-guessing myself. Maybe I pushed too hard to soon.

"I thought I was once, but part of me knew something was off. In the end, I should have listened to my gut. He beat me to within an inch of my life. The experience has made me gun shy. What about you?"

"That's a long story for another day."

"I thought we were sharing and getting to know each other?"

"Come back tomorrow and I promise to share it." She's not saying anything, only drinking her coffee and watching the people.

A few moments pass by before she looks over at me. "Okay, Mick, you've got a deal. Do you have any children?"

"No, and don't try and take the back door, R." She's laughing, and right now that's the best sound in the world.

"That obvious?"

"Yeah."

"Tell me about Covington; I've never heard of it."

"It's a small town in the South. The people are friendly and kind. The food is nothing like you get here."

"How so? I mean, this is New York City, where you can get just about anything at any time of the day or night. I've even had a cup of coffee delivered right to my door!"

"I had a friend in high school who went on to become a Master Chef. He always told me that food should be created from the love in your heart with the skill in your hands. We all thought he was crazy, it took me moving away to finally understand what he meant. Do you cook?"

"Good, God, no and to be honest, I've never had a desire to. What are some of your favorite dishes that you can't get here?"

"Shrimp and grits, gumbo, po-boy, muffulettas, and—for my sweet tooth—beignets."

"I don't think I've ever tried any of them, but I'm sure if we looked hard enough, we could find some of them here."

"What are your favorite foods?"

"Well, coffee and Nutella. After that, nothing really matters. Back to Covington. Tell me more."

"One movie theatre, showing one show daily. There really are no big box stores. There is an old fashioned ice cream parlor across from the train station—best Root beer float ever. A mom and pop type of town."

"Would you have stayed there if you didn't join the Air Force?"

"Yes, my intention was to go back to Covington after I left the Air Force. Sometimes we waste so much time and effort searching for something that was right in front of us the whole time. We just need a kick the teeth to see it."

"That's true, but if you don't venture out, you will never know. I read someplace that we all live and conduct our daily business within a five-mile radius. Sometimes it's healthy to test the waters and see what's waiting for you. Who knows; it could change your life forever."

"Maybe it's true what they say: hind sight is twenty-twenty. Back to you, R, did you know your birth parents?"

"They died when I was young. I have no other family. I had a pretty good childhood. People have had worse. In the end, I survived."

"Tell me about your job. Have you always wanted to teach?"

"Yes, I love working with children. When I see the world through their eyes, it melts my heart. Have you ever heard of the country singer Eric Church?"

"Yes, I'm a big fan of country music. His music has deep meaning."

"He has a song 'Three Year Old.' It's about how everything in life can be learned from a three-year-old. Simple, honesty, life, and love. It gives me hope."

"You're young; you have your whole life ahead of you— never give up hope." We're quite for a while, both of us people watching.

"How long were you deployed?"

"I did six tours. I planned on making it my career."

"Did you go to college or did you just enlist?"

"I went to college, got my Master's degree in Advanced Aviation. From there, I went into officer training school at Maxwell AFB in Alabama. Within nine and a half weeks, I was good to go."

"Maybe you can do something else with your degree."

"All I ever wanted to do was fly. That's no longer an option, now." She takes my hand and gives it a squeeze. I don't even jump at her touch.

"Never give up hope. Everyone has a place. Sometimes that place changes, but don't ever give up. I have faith that you'll find yours. In the meantime, my place is at the gym. I was supposed to meet my roommate thirty minutes ago."

"Tell me about your roommate." I want her to stay.

"That's something for another day. Make sure you stay hydrated. Even though it's a beautiful fall day, it looks like it's going to be a hot one. See you tomorrow, Mick."

I watch her leave, excited and nervous about tomorrow. Hopefully, she shows up.

Chapter Four

Sunday morning church bells are ringing. It's going to be another beautiful day. I hit Starbucks as soon as they open. I want to make sure I'm clean for her. I even shave, thankful for the razor I got at the mission. She's the first friend I've had in a long time and I don't want to blow it.

I get our coffees and go wait on my bench. Every minute feels like an hour. When I look at my watch, it's eleven am. Maybe she forgot, or maybe she changed her mind. This is foolish; why would she want to be my friend? Finally, I see her round the corner. She's all dressed up and when she sees me, she darts across the street.

"Sorry I'm late. Today was pancake Sunday at church. I always help out. I brought you some."

She sits next to me and passes me a container. It's still warm and smells wonderful. "Thank you, did you eat already?"

"Yes, please eat while they're hot."

"Okay, tell me about your roommate while I eat." I pass her a coffee before digging into breakfast.

"His name is Marco. I met him at a soup kitchen when I was fifteen. He left home and was living on the streets."

"Why did he leave home at such a young age?"

"When he told his parents he was gay, they couldn't accept it."

"That's sad; people are who they are. They should be judged on how they treat others, but that's just my own opinion," I offer.

"Tell me about when you fell in love. Don't shake your head you promised."

"R, you drive a hard bargain, but just so you know, you had me with the pancakes." I take a steading breath and begin my story. "Her name was Shay, Shay Davenport. I met her right after I moved to Covington. She was working at the farmer's market, selling corn out of the back of her family's pick-up truck. Before long, I found myself helping out on her family's farm, anything to be close to her. She had three older brothers who watched her every move, and mine. Still, we dated all through high school. We got engaged the night of Senior prom and, when we graduated, we went to a local college. She went for her degree in psychology, since it was her dream to work with children. We were married right before I left."

"So, is she a psychologist with the schools or does she have a private practice?"

"She was a psychologist with Child Protective Services, she was killed by the father of a child she was working with. It happened while I was deployed. I was able to get an emergency leave to go home. But, by the time I got there, her parents had already buried her and, along with her brothers, placed the blame on me."

"Why the hell would they blame you?"

She sounds like a momma bear protecting her young.

"They wanted her to get married and raise a family on their farm. They were not big on the outside world. They felt that I filled her head with all sorts of ideas. They refused to accept that it was Shay's dream to have a career. All she ever talked about was helping children, so I could never understand why they blamed me. You see, that's another reason I could never go back home, they still live there."

"That's just ridiculous; you can't make someone do something they don't want to do. If she would have stayed on the farm, she would have regretted it the rest of her life."

I know what she's saying is true and it's good to hear someone who didn't know her make the same observation.

"We don't have to talk about it, Mick. I don't want you to get upset."

"I think you're the one who's getting upset. It's okay, I've sort of come to terms with it. You would have liked Shay. You kind of remind me of her. She was tough as nails with a heart of gold. I would tease her all the time that she was going to fill our house with babies and puppies."

"It still doesn't make sense to me why they would blame you if she was doing what she loved?"

"They didn't believe in her dream. The only thing they knew was their baby girl was dead and I survived. They needed someone to blame." I close my eyes and fight the bile rising in my throat.

"Maybe we should talk about something else."

"No, I just need a moment." I get up and toss my empty container into the trash. I sit back down and sip my coffee.

"What happened to the guy who murdered Shay?"

"He shot everyone—Shay, the mother, the son, and then, himself."

"That's so horrible. What did you do next?"

"I went back to my unit and, when the time came, I took every mission that was available to me, the more dangerous the better. I didn't care if I lived or died. On my last mission, my plane was shot down. No matter how much I tried to die, God seemed to have a different path in life for me. So here I sit, a little lost and alone."

She turns her head and wipes away a tear that I'm not meant to see. "You're not alone, Mick, you'll always have a friend in me. I never give up; I don't know how."

Her words sink in and I reach over and gently squeeze her hand.

"Mick, if you want to talk about something else, we can."

"No, I'm a man of my word; ask away."

"Yesterday I told you about my last boyfriend and what a disaster that turned out to be. How did you know you loved her, that Shay was the one?"

"There is no standard to gauge love by, so if you're looking for that, you'll never find it. Some people know right away and some over time. For me, it was right away. I walked into that farmer's market and when I got to her truck, she was standing on the tailgate packaging up corn.

She had her beautiful, long, blonde hair in a braid. Her cut-offs a little too short and she was singing along with a song on the radio. I looked over to my best friend Jacob and told him God sent me an angel. He laughed and warned me that her brothers would kill me. I knew, R, right then that was it for me. I needed a purpose, and she was it."

"Do you think people can have a powerful love like that more than once in their lifetime?"

"I can see where you're going with all your questions. Honestly, no. I believe that kind of love is a once in a lifetime thing. I do think there are different types of love, like a love that evolves over time. You always remember your first car, your first kiss . . .your first love."

"Not to change the subject, but I've never had a car."

"Do you at least have a license?" I'm trying to keep the shock out of my voice but I don't think I'm winning.

"Yes, I took driver's education in school. I never had a need for a car. Sorry I digressed; tell me more about Shay. That's such a beautiful name."

I pull a picture out of my wallet and pass it to her. "That's Shay on graduation day from college."

"You're right, she was beautiful."

"I thought it would hurt to talk to you about her, but you make it easy."

"I understand what it feels like to lose someone you love. I also know in time we heal and we're able to remember why we loved them without the pain of the loss. Time really does heal, we only need to open ourselves up to it."

"Why did you choose to talk to me? I mean I'm a homeless guy sitting on a bench. For all you know, I could be dangerous or Lord knows what else."

"I've always given a helping hand when I can. I believe it will come back around somehow. I know what it's like to be scared and alone. I looked into your eyes and I saw someone who was lost not dangerous. So, you finally asked her out . . . continue." She waves her hand and I can't help but laugh, she's like a dog with a bone.

"I started by having lunch with her at school. I worked my way up slowly to asking her out. Since she wasn't allowed to date until she was sixteen, our friends would find ways to get us together. Our first real date was on her sixteenth birthday. I had just gotten my driver's license and my aunt loaned me her car. When I got to her house, the entire family was waiting for me. You can imagine my surprise when they announced they were all coming with us. Shay's mom said birthdays are for family not dates."

"Wow, that must have really burst your bubble." She's laughing and I can laugh at it now but, back then, not so much.

"At first, it did, but after a bit, they made me feel like part of the family. We continued to date and we were even crowned Prom King and Queen."

"I'm sure they knew it was her dream to help children. Maybe they blamed you because they had no one else to blame. Maybe it helped them ease the pain."

"No. They thought she should stay in Covington, get married, and have kids. They were very overprotective of her."

"But that's so old school. Woman can do whatever they want, they shouldn't have to settle," the agitation grows in her voice.

"I agree, but that's the way they viewed it. They thought I was filling her head with fantasies."

"Even after she graduated?"

"Sometimes you have to accept that people will believe whatever they want and nothing you say will change their minds. Anyway, I think I need a break now."

"I'm sorry, I'll let you go."

She gets up to leave and I take her hand to stop her. "Please don't. Let's go for a walk, I need a change of scenery."

"Okay, where would you like to go?"

"I like Central Park, it's a great place to people watch."

"The train is across the street."

She turns to go and I stop dead in my tracks. How do I tell her that I can't go near the train? "I, um, would it be okay if we walk?"

"The park is far from here, is there a problem?"

"I can't take the train. The sound, the smell . . . it's a trigger for me. I'm so sorry." I hope she doesn't leave.

She squeezes my hand and smiles. "Mick, don't worry, I could use the workout, come on."

We walk quietly at first and then she stops and gets hot pretzels and water from a street vendor. We continue the walk as we enjoy them.

"I'm so addicted to these; see, the walk will do me good." She spreads some mustard on a piece before she pops it into her mouth.

"R., you're the nicest person I've met in a long time."

She stops walking, turns towards me and smiles. "Raven, my name is Raven Anderson."

"Raven," I say her name out loud to hear it for myself. I like the way it sounds. "In the sunlight, your hair looks like the color of a Raven." At this mention, she gets a faraway look on her face and continues silently walking. "Did I lose you?"

"Sorry, Mick, I'm still with you. So, back to Shay. How did you handle being separated when you went to flight school?"

"It was only for nine and a half weeks and we were both so busy. She was starting her new job and I was constantly with my head in a book. Once I graduated, I was given my assignment. Whenever I was State side, we were always together. Otherwise, we relied on social media, text, phone and Skype. The relationship worked because we were best friends and we knew what we were both going through. We both knew that I was in the Air force for the long haul. Tell me more about you; I need a break—please. "

We find a bench not too far from the fountain where they filmed friends. It's a beautiful Sunday afternoon and so many people are mulling around the fountain, acting silly.

"Isn't it amazing how many people try to recreate that famous opening scene from friends?"

"Raven, I was here the other day to see Strawberry Fields and someone actually fell in. I had a good Laugh."

"So you want to know more about me. Hmm, well, I work with my best friend Jackie. We were roomies in college; she teaches math."

"Why don't you room with her now?"

"Marco and Jackie don't really get along; they tolerate each other. I had promised Marco we could live together when I graduated. I always keep my word."

"Are you hoping they will somehow grow to like each other?"

"Is it that obvious?"

"Yes, a leopard never changes its spots. Whatever is off between the two of them will always be under the surface. Do you always see the good in everyone?"

"I try, I think that's why I stayed in the bad relationship I was in."

"How were you able to get out? Sometimes it's impossible to get away safely from a violent relationship."

"I was lucky."

I roll my eyes at the notion that getting beat up was lucky.

"I know, Mick, it sounds crazy, even to me, but his reputation was everything to him. He is a doctor and if I pressed charges, he would lose his license. He begged me not to do anything, his parents also pleaded with me. I told him if he left me alone forever and got counseling, I would consider it. I told him if I find out he ever did it again, I would make his life a living hell."

"Do you feel that was the right thing to do? I mean, I'm not judging; I'm just wondering." I'm sure she has a good reason but it seems odd that a woman who is so strong would fold so easily.

"I had to survive and I felt it was my only option. My privacy is everything to me and his family could have tied it up in the courts for a long time."

"How long ago? I mean, you seem skittish when we talk about it."

"It's been eight months. I'm getting back in my groove, but it's slow going. I've also started taking self-defense classes. That's where I went yesterday."

"I'm glad you're taking steps to protect yourself." We get up and stroll through the park again.

"You mentioned you've been out for six months, where have you been?"

"I spent the entire time in rehab at Walter Reed in Bethesda. When they released me, I had no place to go, so I came here. I followed up with the VA hospital when I got here. There's a long wait for services but, like I told you, they did give me a bunch of pamphlets. I also registered with the Department of Veterans Affairs. I'll be okay, it's just going to take time." I'm not sure how convincing I sound but at least I'm trying.

"One day at a time. I need to get going. The school is having a bring a parent to school day next week and then the kids will be getting ready for Halloween. The next couple of weeks will be very busy. I'm going to grab a cab; do you want me to drop you off?"

"No, I'm going to stay here for a while. Be safe and I'll see you tomorrow." She hugs me and I'm taken back. Her friendship is different than anything I've ever experienced before. I watch her leave and then head back to Strawberry Fields. The sun is setting but the park is still bustling with so many families.

Maybe the mission at the Bowery might be worth another try. I've got my meds and as much as I don't want to take them, I would never trust myself without them. I did give up the pain meds. I would rather try and deal with this naturally, rather than having to take the drugs. Everyone who suffers with PTSD deals with it differently. What works for some doesn't always work for others. I hate that people who don't understand it think it's a quick fix: just take a pill to make it all better.

I can't walk to the mission, it's too far and, since the train is not an option, I'll try hailing a cab. So many cabs pass me by that I just about give up when, finally, one of them stops. When I tell him where I want to go, he seems apprehensive. I show him some cash and assure him I can pay. Thankfully, he agrees to take me. He's trying to make conversation but my one word answers seem to convince him that I'd rather have silence. When we pull up, he tells me to keep my money and pay it forward. I thank him for his generosity and reaffirm to him that I will pass it along. I've met so many outstanding people in this city.

I stand outside that red door. It's imposing but, tonight, it's for a different reason. I take a deep breath and this time, I don't hesitate. When I step inside, I'm just in time for Pastor Clarence's sermon. Not everyone believes and not everyone prays to the same God, but I have respect for all religions. Many nights, Shay and I would talk about our beliefs. It was her faith that carried her through the hard times. She was so tender-hearted and sometimes the job overwhelmed her. Not the work, but the children in pain.

When the sermon is done, I sign in for the night. I take my meds and try to relax. No such luck; my mind won't shut off. My heart aches too much for Shay. Why did I make it and she didn't? Did I fail her by not being there to save her?

Once again, I've lost the war—the war within myself. I get up and head into the kitchen. Maybe they'll be setting up for the morning and I can help. When I'm helping someone, I find peace and comfort. However, the only one I find is Pastor Clarence having chocolate chip cookies and milk.

"Mick, you caught me. I'm trying to lose weight but I have a sweet tooth that's not cooperating."

"Well, have you prayed about it?"

He laughs. "Pull up a chair and I'll get you a glass."

The cookies are homemade and dunking them in the cold milk is a little slice of heaven.

"I didn't think I would see you back here so soon, what changed?"

"I made a friend. She's really sweet and she makes me want to try."

"Is she someone that you want to have a relationship with?"

"No, not like you think. She's like a little sister, someone I can talk to. She's not paid to listen and she doesn't judge me. I haven't had that in a long time."

"So, she makes you want to get back into mainstream society. How are you going to do that?"

"One day at a time. Small steps are all I can handle right now and she understands that."

"What made you decide to stay the night?"

"It's one of my baby steps." I push the cookies back toward him.

"Well, Mick, I will be here to help if you need me. Now,

I think I need to step away from the cookies."

"Goodnight and thanks again for being here."

"Always.

I watch him leave and fight the panic I feel rising in my chest. I head back to my cot and once again try to shut off my mind. It's going to be a long night.

Chapter Five

Staring into the darkness, hoping sleep will come . . . nothing. The medication makes my mind react slower, but it still won't shut off. Why, God, did I make it and Shay didn't? What am I supposed to do now? I feel like a compass with a broken needle. I've tried so many things to move forward and heal. Why is it the only thing that seems to help me is talking to Raven? She gives me hope and I can't figure out why.

I close my eyes and start the breathing techniques they taught me at Bethesda. Loving Shay brought out the best part of me. She made it easy for me to try to be a better person. I feel myself finally relaxing. She's in my arms and she's safe. There is no twisting metal, no fire. We're back on the farm, working together. She's eating more blueberries than she's picking. Her lips are stained blue and I can't resist running my tongue over them.

"Oh, baby you taste sweeter than any sugar ever could." I swear I can taste the blueberry on her lips, but I know that's not possible. *We were the king and queen of the prom, if only they could see us now. You're nothing but a memory to them and me. I'm a broken mess. The Air Force called me a hero, they even gave me a medal for rescuing so many people. I'm no hero; I was only doing what anyone in that situation would do—save them. I was fighting to stay alive, but I don't know why when all I wanted was to die so I could be with you.* "Why, Shay, why didn't you fight for me, fight to survive?"

Grief goes in stages or, at least, that's what I've been told. All I know, there's hurt and then more hurt. I need your help, baby, if I'm ever going to survive. You need to show me how. You were always the strong one, help me, Shay, like only you can. I finally drift off to sleep, dreaming of blueberries, lips as sweet as sugar, and all things Shay.

I have no idea how long I slept but, for the first time, I didn't wake up in a panic. No panic attacks, no horrible sounds or smells. As a matter of fact, the only thing I do know is, the sun is shining. When I look around, I realize I'm not at the mission anymore. How is that even possible? I'm in my room at Aunt Beth's house and nothing has changed. Someone keeps beeping a horn and when I look out my window, I see it's Jacob. Maybe I died and this is heaven. Maybe heaven is where you were the happiest on earth, like that movie

Ground Hog Day where you keep reliving the same day over and over again. If Jacob is here, then Shay must be too! I grab my clothes and try to dress as I'm running out the door.

"Jacob, oh my God, I can't believe you're here. Where is Shay?"

"She had to leave early for that special auditorium today. Don't you remember that's why I'm picking up your sorry ass? Maybe if you weren't late coming home from Shay's all the time, your aunt Beth wouldn't have taken away your wheels."

How could this be? Was everything just a bad dream? Have I been living in a nightmare all this time?

"Come on, man, can't you drive any faster? I really need to see Shay."

"If I get another ticket, my dad will take the keys, then what will we do?"

He pulls into the school parking lot and I'm running out of the car before he even stops. I've got to see if this is real, if she's really alive. I race through the auditorium doors and she's here—she's really here! Maybe this is real? Maybe the war was only a nightmare, a look at what's to come if I join the Air force.

"Shay, you're here!"

"Of course I'm here. Are you okay?"

"I had the worst dream ever." *I pull her into my arms and hold her so tight. I don't want to let her go. If I do, she could vanish. I could wake up and she could be gone.*

"Mick, I can't breathe, and I need to finish setting up for the assembly." *I ease up and when she looks up at me with those beautiful blue eyes, I kiss her. I don't care how much trouble we will get in to; I need to feel her sweet lips on mine.*

"Mick Callan, you're going to get us both in trouble. Now, I really have to finish setting up. Classes start in five minutes, so you better get going." She gives me a quick peck on the cheek and runs back on stage. *I don't care about classes; I don't care about anything but her.*

"Callan, shouldn't you be heading to class now?" the familiar bellow from principal Sanders echoes throughout the auditorium and, right now, I welcome it.

"Yes, Mr. Sanders, on my way now, sir." I head out to my physics class, excited in the knowledge that this is reality and everything else was just a sick and twisted nightmare. I'm racing down the hall but it seems to get darker. It's like standing outside, trying to look through a dirty window. I try to run back to the auditorium but there is nothing but blackness. I try running toward the little bit of light that's left but my feet won't move. Finally, it's gone and I'm surrounded by an eerie darkness. I've drifted back into my hell.

Chapter Six

I feel someone tugging at my arm, but I don't want to open my eyes. I want to say here forever. Maybe if I wait it out, she will come back. I'm trying to reach for something to hold on to, anything. I hear a familiar voice but not from my past.

"Mick, it's time to wake up. The daily sermon is going to start in ten minutes."

My eyes fly open and my hand is around Pastor Clarence's throat.

"Oh my God, I'm so sorry, sir." I let go and my whole body begins to shake and sweat. With my stomach in knots, I jump up and run to the men's room. I know I'm going to vomit, but nothing comes, only the shakes and some dry heaves. I curl up in a ball on the floor with my head between my knees, rocking and praying for this nightmare to end.

"Please, God, please let me go from this hell. I don't know why you saved me. I'm no good to anyone, least of all myself. I'm broken and useless; how could anyone love me when I can't even love myself? I wasn't there for Shay when she needed me the most. Even with all my training, I couldn't save Dominic. What the hell am I good for?"

I don't expect him to answer me, he never does. I don't know how much time has passed, but I know I can't stay on this floor. I try to pull myself together and at least make it to the sink to wash up. The cold water on my face feels good until I look at my reflection in the mirror. The man staring back at me frightens me. "Shake it off, Mick." Great, now I'm talking to myself. When I look at my watch, I realize I missed the only bright spot in my life right now: coffee with Raven. I fight the pity party I feel myself falling into. I go back to my cot and get dressed before heading out to apologize to Pastor Clarence.

When I slip into the sanctuary, he's just finishing up, and I take a seat in the back. After everyone files out, he takes a seat next to me. "I'm sorry, sir. I'll get my stuff and leave." My head is down and I can't seem to bring myself to face him. Maybe it's the shame, embarrassment, or lack of self-control that I feel, or maybe it's the fear of what I'll see in his eyes when I do: pity.

He puts his hand on my shoulder. "Mick, please look at me."

When I finally find the courage to look at him, all I see is kindness. A man who wants nothing more than to take my pain away.

"Last night you told me that staying here was a baby

step. No one said this would be easy, but at least you're try-ing. I knew you weren't going to hurt me. You can't give up, son, you've got to keep trying."

"How did you know?" My voice is barely a whisper.

"I have faith."

Right now, he has more faith in me than I do. "Well, thank you for believing in me, but I can't take a chance that it could happen again."

"If you give up now, then everything, up till now, would've been a waste of time. And, what about your friend you told me about? Are you going to give up on her, too?"

"I was a fool to think I could have a friendship with her. I'm too messed up . . . too broken. Hell, I can't even spend six hours sleeping in the safety of this mission without try-ing to strangle the Pastor! I don't trust myself anymore. This is what's become of me." I close my eyes and silently pray for some sort of divine intervention.

"What did you do differently last night that made you think you would be able to sleep here?"

"I took some of my meds."

"Mick, I'm no doctor, but I don't think you can take them only when you choose too. If you don't mind me ask-ing, why did you only take some of them?"

"I don't take the pain meds. I don't like the way they make me feel. As an alternative, I try to do Yoga and a series of breathing techniques I learned at Bethesda. I only take the antidepressants when I feel I really want to try for a normal life. We all know how that worked out."

"Well, like I said, I'm no doctor, but you might want to think about following the directions on your medications.

In the meantime, how about you stay here today and help me with a small project I'm working on."

"Why? I mean, if you genuinely need help with something, I'm more than happy to help, but if you're afraid I'm going to do something to harm myself, don't be."

He turns, puts his hand on my shoulder, and gives it a squeeze. "I'm asking you to stay because I need help with a project, nothing more."

I get up and offer him my hand. "Lead the way."

The mission has so many different rooms and each one is being utilized for different things: classrooms, meetings, or just for storage. When we get to a huge room with only one small folding table, Pastor Clarence steps inside, picks up a folder, and hands it to me. "Mick, the mission gets a lot of donations. At first, we kept them in a small room and when someone needed something, we would rummage through the stuff and get them what they needed. Organization has never been my strong suit but, with the amount of donations that we get, this room is filled to capacity. I want to turn it into a small thrift store." He waves his hand around the old, dusty room, giving me a chance to take it all in. "We will still give to people in need, but if we could resell some of the stuff, that money could go into other programs. A local builder donated some supplies, but what I need is someone to put it all together." He presses a folder into my hands. "This folder has the building plans. You wouldn't be working alone; there are a few more men here that are good with their hands. Do you think this is something you can help with?"

I helped Shay's brothers build a barn and a little farm

stand type of store, I'm sure I can easily do this. "I would be happy to help you build this. When do you want me to start?"

"No time like the present. All the supplies are in the adjoining room and, when you're ready, I can send some men back to help you. I'll leave you to get started." He heads out the door and I could swear I hear him chuckle. I look through the folder and now I know why he was laughing. His building plans read like an IKEA how-to manual that's gone awry. I don't think IKEA could even put this together. I check out the building supplies that were donated and there is more than enough to get this job done. Right now, I don't need anyone to help me. After a good cleaning, I can start repairing the drywall and then paint. It's not going to take that long to build shelving. There's also a display case that can hold the smaller stuff.

After several hours, I'm up on the ladder, finishing the last of the work for today, when I hear a knock on the door. I glance over my shoulder. Standing in the doorway is one of the volunteers with a plate of food. "Hi, I'm Cathy. Pastor Clarence said you need to take a break and eat. I thought I would bring it to you while it's still hot."

I climb down from the ladder and take the tray from her. "Thank you."

"So, how long have you been in town?"

"A couple of weeks." I'm not in the mood for idol chit-chat but I also don't need to be rude to her.

"I was born and raised right here in New York City. Where did you come from?"

Great, just what I need today—Chatty Cathy. "A small

town in the south. Thanks for bringing me some food, I better eat it while it's still hot." She's not taking the hint; she leans against the wall and smiles.

"I can stay and keep you company while you eat."

"Thanks, but I'm going to eat while I work. I really want to get the painting started." Please, Chatty Cathy, take the hint.

"Okay, I'll be here again tomorrow. I usually only volunteer one day a week, but they are short-staffed here, so I'm going to be picking up the slack."

Oh joy. "That's very nice of you. Thanks again for the food." I climb up the ladder and get back to work. I hear the door close and finally, I'm alone. I'm better off by myself, lost in my work.

Hours go by like minutes and I realize it's getting dark. I take stock of everything I've accomplished today and I feel better—not great—but better. I'm cleaning up, when Pastor Clarence comes in.

"Mick, were you trying to get it all done in one day?"

"Time got away from me and it's not like I've got anything better to do."

"Will you be staying for the service and spending the night?"

"I'll stay for the service. I'm not sure about spending the night."

"Do you want my opinion?"

I have to laugh. "Sir, you'll give it either way." He's laughing with me and it's nice to hear.

"I think you should stay the night. Take your meds again. Maybe being more consistent will help you. If you really fear that you might hurt someone, bring a cot in this room. At least you'll be safe."

"I'll think about it, promise."

We head to the Sanctuary and, thankfully, Chatty Cathy is gone for the night. Maybe he's right, maybe I should keep taking the meds and try to sleep inside, rather than on a park bench. Maybe if I take the meds, I will be back with Shay. Maybe if I stay asleep forever, I can be with Shay. Who am I kidding? It was just a dream, a damn realistic one, but still just a dream. I'm trying to stay focused on the sermon but my mind keeps drifting to the possibility of seeing Shay. Pastor Clarence ends with a quote from Mathew 11:28. *"Come to me, all who labor and are heavy laden, and I will give you rest."*

His words seem to pull me in and always pack a punch. Everyone files out but I hang back.

"Mick, what did you think of tonight's sermon?"

"I think you were aiming at me tonight."

His hearty chuckle fills the quiet room. "Maybe just a bit. Did it work?"

"I'm going to stay here tonight but I'm bringing my cot into the back room."

"I'll meet you in the kitchen for some cookies and milk."

"Guess that diet thing is a bust."

"I've been praying about it. Maybe if I eat one less cookie tonight, it will be a good start. Kind of like you trying to start again."

"Maybe you should consider going into politics?"

"Only to clean it up, Mick."

True to his word, Pastor Clarence ate one less cookie. I'm lying here in the dark, waiting for my meds to kick in. Am I doing this so I get a chance to see Shay again or do I really want to have a life? There's no guarantee that I will even see my beautiful wife or taste those lips that are sweeter than blueberries.

My mind wanders as I try to relax. I missed having coffee with Raven today. Maybe it's for the best; getting close to anyone right now doesn't seem like a smart move. I know we all carry baggage in life but the little bit she shared with me is more baggage than anyone should have to carry.

I close my eyes and start the meditation techniques. Trying to organize all the clutter that's in my head. Putting it all into little compartments. Finally, I feel my mind start to relax and drift off to sleep.

I'm wet, everything around me is wet, and when I open my eyes, I'm standing in the shower at my aunt's house. How could this be? There's a banging on the door and it snaps me out of my confusion.

"Mick, if you don't hurry up you'll be late for the prom."

Aunt Beth? Prom? How is any of this even possible? I shut the water and pull the curtain back. Sure enough, I'm in Aunt Beth's house in Covington. I must be going insane. Maybe I'm being given a second chance, a chance to right all the wrongs. I finish up and head into my bedroom. Sure enough, my tux is hanging on my closet door. Is God giving me a chance to relive the best moments of my life? Is that why this is happening? I don't care if it's only in my mind, I want this so badly that nothing is going to stand in my way, not even reality.

I'm all dressed, staring at myself in the mirror, wondering about tonight. I pat the ring in my pocket and head out to pick up Shay. Tonight's the night. We've waited to be together, but tonight will be different.

When I get to the farm to pick her up, her dad and brothers are waiting for me. I wanted to tell them my plan. Maybe do the traditional thing and ask them for permission to marry Shay, but the truth is, no matter what they say it wouldn't matter. I love her with all of my heart and soul. Nothing can ever change that, nothing. As they begin issuing me all sorts of warnings, Shay comes down the steps. Everything around me sounds like Charlie Brown noise. There's a loud pounding in my ears. All I see is an angel, my love, my Shay. She has on a beautiful, blue, strapless gown that matches her eyes. I'm glad I listened to Jacob and got a wrist corsage. With trembling hands, I slip it on her wrist. Hopefully, I won't be trembling so much when I slip the ring on her finger.

"You're so beautiful." I can barely get the words out; all I want to do is take her in my arms and hold her forever.

"Thank you. We better get going or we'll be late."

Her mom takes all kinds of pictures and then we head out. Finally, we're on our way. When we get to the dance, Jacob and his date, Wendy, are waiting for us.

"I swear, Mick, you're always late. If Jacob was late like that all the time, I think I would strangle him."

"Hey, quit giving me grief; you know Shay's house is the furthest from town. We better get inside before they close the

doors."

Shay steps inside and I'm about to go in when the doors close. They're locked. I'm banging and yelling for someone to let me in. Someone is yelling my name, over and over again.

"Mick, are you okay? Mick, please open the door."

When I open my eyes, I'm on my cot at the mission. I hear Chatty Cathy on the other side of the door. Of all people to drag me back to this hell.

"I'm fine, just waking up," I yell back at her. I don't want to see anyone right now, least of all the busy body. I wait and when I finally hear her walk away, I gather my stuff and head to the showers. Maybe I can still catch Raven. Maybe she can make some sense out of this.

Chapter Seven

I'm heading to my bench and when I look at my watch, I realize I'm probably too late. That is, until I turn the corner and find her sitting there with two coffees.

"Raven, I'm sorry I missed you yesterday and now today I'm late." Before I can say anything more, she puts the coffees down, gets up, and gives me a hug. I'm startled but I don't shy away from it.

"I'm sorry. I have been so worried about you and then I realized you have no way to get in touch with me." She presses a piece of paper into my hand.

"That's my cell. If you ever need me, please call. Don't wait till I get here." She waves her hand over the bench and when we sit down, she hands me a coffee.

"I've been at the mission. I've been helping out there and stayed the past two nights. "

"Wow, so you're able to stay inside? That's great."

"Not really. I have so much to tell you but I know you have to go to school."

"Actually, it's a delayed start day. If you don't mind walking with me, we can talk along the way."

We get up and start walking. I thought I could tell her everything but what if she thinks I'm nuts? Hell, at this point, I think I'm nuts. "I don't know where to begin."

"Well, how about you start with what brought you to the mission and then you can tell me what happened when you were there."

"I heard about the mission from one of the pamphlets I got. I went once and listened to Pastor Clarence speak; he really hit the mark with his sermon. He let me shower and gave me a hot meal. When you left me at the park the other day, I felt something that I haven't felt in a long time."

"What's that?"

"Hope."

She stops and closes her eyes. She's not moving or saying anything. Finally, she opens her eyes, looks at me and smiles. "It's nice to know that I can help just by listening. Please continue."

"From the first day we met, you never judged me. I like our friendship, you're like a little sister that I never had. I wanted to try and see if I could eventually get my own place and work myself back into mainstream society. I thought if I took my meds then maybe I could try and sleep inside."

"I think you should be taking your meds on a daily basis. Anyway, how did you make out?"

"Well, not very good, I woke up with my hands around Pastor Clarence's throat."

"Oh no, is he okay?"

"Yes, he's fine. I, on the other hand, became ill at the thought that I might have hurt someone who was only trying to help me."

We get to her school and there's a bench across from the playground. We sit and now I have to tell her the hardest part.

"You seem apprehensive about finishing your story, Mick, why?"

"You might think I'm nuts. I promise I'm not but I don't know why this is happening."

"Why what's happening?"

I'm trying not to make myself sick. I take a few steading breaths and continue. "I fell asleep and I was reliving some of my life with Shay. It was so real, I could taste the sweet blueberries on her lips. I thought I was going crazy."

"Do you think it was some sort of hallucination? Could it be a side effect from your meds?"

"Honestly, I didn't know what to think. Pastor Clarence wanted me to stay again last night but I was apprehensive about it. I was afraid I might hurt someone. He suggested that I take my cot and go sleep in the room I've been renovating into a thrift store for the mission. I said okay."

She holds up her hand to stop me. "Wait, tell me the truth; did you say yes because you were hoping to get back to that time when Shay was alive or did you really want to try and have some sort of future?"

I'm kicking at the dirt between the stones, embarrassed to tell her the truth, but I know I must. "I thought if I keep taking my meds, I might be able to keep seeing Shay.

Maybe if I took them all, I might never have to leave her." I can barely get the words out; my stomach is in knots. She's holding my hand and squeezing it so tight.

"Mick, I know in your heart you think this is real, that seeing Shay is real, but it's not. Our mind can play tricks on us. I know this from experience. I don't usually share this with anyone but if it will help you, then it's worth it." She closes her eyes and takes a deep breath. When she opens them, she seems so sad. "My birth father was an FBI agent and when I was a little girl, I was kidnapped. When my father and his partner rescued me, my father was shot and killed right in front of me. For a long time, I believed he would visit me at night. It got to the point where I wouldn't speak, ever. It was only with therapy and time that I was able to make a separation from what was real and what I wanted to be real. Do you know how sad I would be if you were gone? You need to understand that you matter, Mick."

I can't believe what I'm hearing. "Raven, I look at you and you seem so together, yet everything you've been through should have torn you apart. How do you continue to carry on and see the bright side of life?"

"I'm not always so together. I have my moments when I just want to have a pity party, but then I realize I can't go back. No matter how much you try, the past is behind you for a reason. God chose you to survive for a reason. I think the first thing you need to do is see a doctor. Maybe your meds need to be changed, but you'll never know that if you keep trying to play doctor!"

The bell is ringing and the kids on the playground are lining up to go inside. I know she has to go, I just wish she didn't have to.

"I have to go, but promise me you will meet me here at four o'clock. Don't even think of arguing."

"I will be here, promise."

She gets up, runs through the playground and in the back door. I'm left sitting here, wondering how easy she made it for me to promise to be here.

I have some time before I have to meet her, so I head to the postal place to check my box. There is some mail from my bank, confirming that I changed my address. The rest is all junk mail. I swear that crap follows me faster than anything else. With the weather getting cooler, I find a place to get some warmer clothes. I work my way toward the school and pick her up a pretzel and a bottle of water. I know I'm really early but when I get there, she's sitting on the bench, waiting.

"Hey, I thought I was really early. What are you doing here now?"

"I got out early."

She's not looking me and her cheeks are flushed. "Raven, did you leave work early because you were worried about me?"

"Yeah, I was worried. I called the VA hospital and I think I have scared the living daylights out of everyone there. Apparently, they hold back some appointments for emergencies. You have to be there in an hour, so we need to leave now."

"What would you have done if I didn't come back here early?"

"I didn't think it all the way through. All I knew is that you needed to get in to see someone today. Now, we need to get going." She steps into the street and hails a cab and, of course, one stops for her right away. This time of day, traffic isn't so bad.

"What did you do today after I left you?"

I pass her the water and pretzel. "You'll be happy to know that I went to check my mail and my junk mail has followed me." She looks at me and gets hysterical laughing.

"Isn't it funny how sometimes the government can't find its way out of a paper bag, but junk mail will find us even if we were on Mars?"

The cab driver begins telling her about all the junk mail he gets and how he shreds it and recycles it by putting it in his son's hamster's cage. She has been in this man's company for five minutes and he's telling her his whole life story. I swear she's got a gift that makes people feel so comfortable with her. Our driver lets us out right at the front entrance and we head inside. I'm nervous about being here, but Raven takes the lead and finds out exactly where we need to be.

"Will you come in the waiting room with me?" I'm nervous and, at this point, I'm not ashamed to ask her for support.

"I will do whatever you need me to. You have to make me one promise. You have to tell the doctor everything, not just what you think he wants to hear."

"Okay, you've got a deal."

We step inside the packed room. "It's very crowded; maybe we should come back another day." She takes ahold of my arm and squeezes.

"Tomorrow will be the same as today." Guess I've got no choice. Now, we wait. To my surprise, they call my name pretty quickly and I head back. The nurse makes everything seem pretty routine until she gets to the part about my meds.

"Do you have a problem taking them as prescribed?"

"I was never a fan of medication and this stuff makes me feel weird," I try to explain it to her.

She nods her head while typing, God knows what, into the computer. Finally, she stops and gives me her attention. "Okay, the doctor should be in in a few moments." She steps out, leaving me to wait, and boy am I waiting. Thirty minutes pass. I'm about to get dressed and leave when there's a knock on the door and the doctor comes in.

"Hello, Mr. Callan, I'm Dr. Simpson. Why don't you tell me what's going on while I examine you?"

He's doing a quick exam while I go into details about the past two days and then giving him the express version on Shay's murder and my plane crash. "I'm not sure if these are dreams or hallucinations. Sometimes I feel like I'm able to relive them and other times I feel like I'm looking at them from the outside."

"Mr. Callan, first, you must take your medicine as prescribed, otherwise, how will you know if it works or not? Second, it is not unusual with PTSD to have nightmares that bring you back to the incident that might have caused it. You think it was your plane crash but what if it was when your wife was murdered? What if you have survivor's guilt and your dreams are leading you up to that day so you can try and change history? There are so many 'what if's.'"

"I thought that's why I was here . . . so you could tell me why this is happening?"

"The brain is a funny thing, not ha-ha funny but an odd funny; it has its safety mechanisms. We can work on this together, but you must promise me you will take your medication, otherwise, I can't help you. Now, what I will do today is change the dosage to something that might be more manageable for you. I think you might be better served with Cognitive Processing Therapy. I will have the nurse set up an appointment right away, so you can get started. I believe if you can work through the events of your life leading up to today, you might be able to gain more control. You have to remember, you can't change the past no matter how much you want to. The nurse will give you the information packet on Cognitive Processing Therapy for you to review. If it doesn't work, don't get discouraged; there are many other options we can try."

"Do you think I can be fixed?" He's the first person I've ever asked this. I never really wanted to be fixed; I only wanted to be with Shay.

"What kind of doctor would I be if I didn't think I could help you? You're not a broken man, you just have a few kinks in your armor that you need to get worked out. You need a helping hand, and I'm here to give it to you. Now, I also want to draw some blood. The lab is at the end of the hall and when you check out, the nurse will make that appointment for you. One day at a time; keep telling yourself that." He shakes my hand and walks out. For the first time in months I feel like I have some hope.

I get everything squared away with the nurse and the tech in the lab got me on one stick. When I get back to the waiting area, Raven is talking to three different people. She sees me, says her goodbyes, and we head outside.

"Well, I'm busting here; what happened? If it's too personal, you don't have to tell me."

"For the first time, I have hope. He's a nice guy and not a know-it-all type of doctor. He changed the dosage on my medication and he set me up with Cognitive Processing Therapy. Let's grab some coffee and we can go through these brochures together. That is . . . if you have the time."

"Of course I have the time for you!"

We find a Starbucks, which is not hard to do in this town, and snag a table in the back where it's quiet. I give her the brochures while I get the coffee.

"Mick, this is very interesting. It is divided into four parts. The first part is learning about PTSD. The second helps you become more aware of your thoughts and feelings. The third is learning coping skills and, finally, the fourth is the change in beliefs after going through the trauma. When is your appointment?"

"Tomorrow at ten." I'm staring at the information but lost in my own thoughts.

"You're going, right?"

She's more demanding than asking and I have to laugh. I look at her like a little sister but, in reality, she's my saving grace. "Do you think this will work?"

"You have to have hope and believe that it will work. You have to be open to try, otherwise, you will always wonder 'what if' and that's not something you want to live with. You must go in there with an open heart and an open mind. Nothing else will do. Do you want me to go with you?"

"No, you've done so much already. I promise I will keep the appointment."

"I need to get going. Do you want to share a cab?"

"No, I'm going to go back to the mission and continue my work on the thrift store."

"Do you want to meet tomorrow when school lets out?"

"Yes, I'll be on the bench across from the playground," I agree. She gets up, gives me a hug, and heads out. I review the information one more time before heading back to the mission.

Chapter Eight

The mission is packed; the colder the weather gets the more people are seeking shelter and a hot meal. How sad that so many people in this country are in need of some sort of help. I jump right into my work and the shop is really shaping up. So far, no sign of Chatty Cathy, so that's good. I've got all the shelving up and the counter is next. I haven't been working that long but It's almost time for dinner, so I'll wait to start it. Instead, I decide to clean up and head out to the dining room in case they need some help.

Pastor Clarence is trying to work two food stations, so I jump right in and take over one of them. "Mick, thank you, I didn't know you were here."

"I went directly into the store, so I could get some more work done before dinner. I should have it all done tomorrow."

"Wow, that's great. I knew you were a God send."

Chatty Cathy comes rushing in the door, seemingly all flustered. She jumps on the line and takes over for Pastor Clarence. She's not her usual chatty self and her eyes are puffy, like she's been crying. When we finally get everyone through the line, I make a dish for myself before breaking down my station. I look over at Cathy and she's staring at an empty chafing dish in front of her. "Cathy, what's wrong," I ask. She jumps at my words.

"My husband's job is transferring him to a different location, so we have to move. It's not the first time but it never gets easy. We've been here the longest and the kids and I have made some great friendships."

"Your friends don't go away just because you move."

"I'm not worried about me; it's the kids I'm worried about. They are both in High School and they are not happy about all of this."

"I had to move to a different state when I was thirteen, so I understand how they must feel. When do you have to move?"

"He has to be there in two weeks, I'll wait until Christmas break and then they can start the first of the year."

I make her a dish of food and then help her break down her station. "I'm sure it will all work out. Let's eat before the sermon starts."

Once again, Pastor Clarence's message hits home. It's like he can get inside of me, to the darkest parts of my soul. I hang back, straighten out the room and wait for him.

"I missed you this morning and yet you managed to still get so much done on the store. Did you have a good day?"

"The friend I told you about took me to see a doctor today."

He sits down and pats the chair next to him. "I'm very proud of you; taking that first step was huge."

"I fight my inner demons every day but at least I know I'm not alone. I'm going to start a special therapy program tomorrow. I talked to the doctor about the medication. He lowered the dosage and made me promise to take it every day."

"I know how hard that first step is. I was once in your shoes. I was in the Army in Vietnam and when I finally made it back home, everyone moved on without me. I was drafted to fight in a war that no one wanted. When I came home, the very people I was trying to protect hated me. It took a long time for me to get to the other side of this. We didn't have that many services available to us. PTSD was very misunderstood and the only solace I found was in a bottle. Eventually, I found someone who offered me a hand up, not a handout. That's when I realized my best work would be here, helping others."

He closes his eyes and takes a deep breath. It's at this moment I realize he's just as human as the rest of us. We can stumble, we can fall, but we still get up every day and try all over again. That's all anyone can ask for. And, who knows, maybe—just maybe—one of those times, we will be successful.

"Thank you, sir, for sharing your experiences with me."

"Every morning that you get up, and make it through the day, puts you one step closer to being whole again."

"Would it be okay if I stayed, again?"

"Of course. Let's finish cleaning up here and I will meet you later for cookies and milk."

"How's that working out for you, sir?" I'm trying not to laugh.

"Well, tonight I will be down to two cookies. If I can get to one a day, I'll be a happy man."

I head back to the store to start work on the counter. I put the country music station on the radio and before I know it, I'm lost in my work. I think I'm doing great until Cole Swindell starts singing "You Should Be Here." I know I should shut it off, but I can't. When I open my eyes, I think of her. And, when I fall asleep at night, she's all I see. "Oh, Shay, why?"

I hear someone clear their throat and when I turn around, Pastor Clarence is standing in the doorway. "Mick, it's getting late; I'll help you clean up in here."

Glancing at my watch, I realize it's almost midnight. "I'm sorry. I wanted to get this counter finished before I went to bed."

"I'm truly amazed by your work. You're good with your hands. Maybe that's what you should be doing."

"I've never thought about it. All I ever wanted to do was fly."

"You never know what kind of impact you're going to have on someone's life. I have faith that you'll find where you're supposed to be and what you're supposed to be doing, and when you do, it will hit you like a brick between the eyes."

"Well, I hope not! Come on, sir, let's go have those

cookies before they're all gone."

True to his word, he had one less cookie tonight. I kept my promise, as well, and took my medication. He heads to bed and I head into the showers. I want to fall asleep. I want to see her again, though I know it's not real. Maybe I'm trying to right some wrong but what that wrong is, I don't know. I really hope the therapy works. Living like this is not living; I exist in a hell that I wouldn't wish on anyone. My cot is all set up and now I start my nightly meditation, trying to calm my racing heart. The next thing I know, Shay is pulling me toward the dance floor.

"Mick, you're not getting out of this. You promised if we won, you would dance with me. Mr. Sanders is getting ready to announce the winners."

I don't think we won, but she swears she has a good feeling about this. Sure enough, Sanders calls our names. I spin her around in my arms and then take her on to the dance floor. All eyes are on us as the DJ plays "Where were you (When the World Stopped Turning)" by Alan Jackson.

I've been practicing with Aunt Beth for two weeks and all my hard work has paid off. There could be a thousand people in the room but, right now, it's just us.

"I love you, Shay," my voice barely a whisper. Before the song is over, the DJ invites everyone up to dance. With the ring practically burning a hole in my pocket, the timing is perfect for me to whisk her out of there.

"Mick, why are we leaving?"

"I have a surprise for you, but we need to leave now."

"Are you going to at least give me a clue?"

"If I give you a clue and you guess, you'll get pissed at

me."

"You know me so well."

She's laughing but the truth is I really want to surprise her and if I wait any longer, I'm not sure I will be able to keep this secret. The drive to the Garden District doesn't take that long and when I pull up in front of the mansion, she squeals.

"Oh my God, you didn't?"

"Yes, I did. You've been talking about this place for as long as I know you. I finally saved up enough to get us dinner and a room overnight. If I could give you the world, babe, I would."

Back in the day, this mansion was someone's home. It's been completely renovated and turned into a hotel. The new owners kept all the details that made this home unique. When we step inside, she stops and looks at me with tears in her eyes. "This is so spectacular and I can't believe you were able to pull this off."

"Come on, we have a dinner reservation and afterwards, I want to show you the grounds." We head into the dining room and the hostess escorts us to a table on the back patio. Watching her in the moonlight is like watching an angel. When I made the reservation, I told the hostess what I was planning and she had the chef make up a personalized menu with our names are printed across the top. Each new dish is better than the last. When it finally came to dessert the only thing I asked for was fresh blueberries to be incorporated into the dish, and the chef didn't disappoint.

"I can't believe we're really here. This is so amazing, and the food is a work of art. Each dish more beautiful than the last. I've eaten stuff tonight that I never heard of."

I'm watching her enjoy the chocolate crepes filled with blueberries and all I want to do is kiss her.

"Mick, are you going to have some of this or just watch me eat it?"

"Sorry, I was daydreaming about those beautiful lips and how much I want to kiss them."

"Well, why don't you?"

I quickly get up and offer her my hand. "Why don't we tour the gardens." I know exactly where I want to go and lead her in the direction of the fountain. There are gardenia bushes everywhere and the smell is intoxicating.

With my hand wrapped around the ring in my pocket, I gather up my courage and begin, "Shay." What the hell is that buzzing sound? Oh no, not now please not now. I open my eyes and I'm back at the shelter with the alarm on my phone going off. I was so close . . . close to having her again. I close my eyes and try to get back to that moment but I can't. She has slipped through my fingers, yet again. "Why, God . . . why are you doing this to me? What is the lesson I'm supposed to learn?" Nothing but silence, a deafening silence. I get up and get ready for my appointment.

Chapter Nine

I don't want to be late for my appointment, so I grab a coffee and head to the bus stop. The long bus ride gives me the time to think and people watch. I'm nervous about today. Maybe I'm grasping at straws, trying to find an alternative type of treatment. Even if I find a way to cope with the PTSD, what will I do with my life? Raven told me that there is something out there for me but, honestly, I can't see it. I have one more stop to go but traffic is at a dead stop. I get off and walk the rest of the way.

When I finally find the right office, everything is a hurry up and wait while I fill out numerous papers that are basically saying the same thing over and over again. No wonder people get so disgusted with doctors. I look around and there are quite a few Veterans here. Aunt Beth always said service men and women stand out in a crowd even when they're not in uniform. I never quite understood what she meant until now. We are called back as a group and as I follow everyone in. The urge to bolt gets stronger. Sweat is beginning to bead up on my neck and every smell is becoming more intense. The touch of the nurses hand on my arm makes me leap, snapping me back to the here and now.

"Mr. Callan, the first step is the hardest. There's coffee and water in the back of the room. Help yourself to some. This first meeting is for educational purposes only, that's why it's done in a group setting. After that, your sessions will be one on one."

I take a seat closest to the door, just in case the need to bolt becomes too much. Part of me wishes I could have Raven here with me, but the other part of me never wants to expose her to all of this. Finally, a man comes in and introduces himself as a psychiatrist and begins to explain, in great detail, the twelve-week process. I don't understand how it's possible to help me in such a short amount of time. I'm not sure if I'm staying because I promised Raven or if I really want help.

Two hours later, armed with a mountain of information and a headache to match, I've got my first appointment done. I have time before I have to meet Raven, and I need something to eat. I head toward her school and find a place called The Shake Shack. I think I might have died and gone to heaven. Aside from the best bacon cheeseburger I've ever had, they have a hometown favorite: Abita draft root beer. I get two bottles and put one in my backpack for Raven. My headache is starting to disappear; it's time to look at my homework. It looks like a waste of time, but I never break a promise. I gather everything up and head toward the school. If ever I needed some sort of encouragement, now's the time.

I get to the school just as the bell rings. It's the first time I take notice of all the plain clothes security around the school. If they want to blend in, they aren't doing a very good job. Suits, dark glasses, and ear pieces are all a dead giveaway. All of the staff is helping direct the students and when they are all gone, Raven comes running over.

"Sorry I'm late, everyone seemed to be moving at a snail's pace today. How did the appointment go?"

"It was overwhelming and I have homework. The first appointment was done in a group session. All the others will be one on one with the doctor."

"I'm proud of you."

"Really?"

"Like Martin Luther King Jr. said 'Faith is taking the first step even when you don't see the whole staircase.'"

I wish I had as much faith in myself as she does. Maybe in time things will become clearer for me.

"I had the most unbelievable lunch today and I brought you something." I quickly pull the bottle of root beer out of my backpack. "This is a hometown favorite. I can't believe they sell it at The Shake Shack."

"Oh, I've been there, they have the best chicken sandwich ever. Sometimes Jackie and I go there cause they make a portabella shroom meatless burger that she loves. So what kind of homework do you have?"

"I have to write an impact statement. It will help give the doctor a baseline of my understanding of what happened and why."

64

"Are you okay with that?"

"No. I realized today that I have to be really truthful with myself if I'm ever going to have a shot at this working. It's more than just one thing. If I could say my world changed when my plane crashed then that would be fine, I could work forward from that point. The truth is, Shay's murder and her parents blaming me for it is a big part of it. There's so much that I have to live with and take responsibility for. How can I possibly put this all into a statement?"

She takes my notes and begins flipping through them. "Your notes say the impact statement should be brief. Then you put the details into a journal. You'll have to read the doctor the journal out loud. When is this due?"

"My appointment is Friday."

"Okay, that gives us a few days. Maybe we need to break it down into smaller sections. Since Shay's death is huge for you, start at the end and work your way backwards. Start with the plane crash and let's work back from there. You're going to have to bring yourself mentally to the morning of the crash."

She pulls out a notebook from her bag, and takes another sip of the root beer. Now she's all ready to take notes for me.

"I'll put all of your notes in this notebook and you can also use it as your journal. I'll also make notes on a separate sheet of paper for you to use as your impact statement. Close your eyes and picture the morning of the crash. How did you start that day?"

I close my eyes and rub my temples, trying to ward off the pounding in my head. "It starts out just like any other day. My alarm goes off at five am. I get up make the bed and head into the shower. Get dressed and get some coffee. I go into my mission planning meeting to get my objective and then I head out to my aircraft. I do the standard walk around to start my inspections. When I finish on the outside I climb inside to start my checklist." My mind flashes back to that morning on the tarmac. I can hear the blood pounding in my ears. I'm trying to slow down my breathing, but now I feel the sweat start to bead on the back of my neck.

"Take a break if you need to."

I don't want to take a break I just want this over. I keep rubbing my temples, I take a deep breath and continue. "We weren't that long into the mission when we were hit by something. I'm not sure what the hell it was; all I know is I feel the heat . . . intense, burning heat." I get up and race to the trash can. *So much for my wonderful lunch.* When I catch my breath, I sit back down, my head in my hands and sweat is now running down my chest. I can hear the rustling of Raven's bag. I lift my head out of my hands just as she pulls a bottle of water out and passes it to me, along with a hand wipe.

"That's some bag of tricks you've got there."

"Mick, I'm a teacher; you can't begin to image what I can pull out of that bag. Take your time; we're not in a rush." She's rubbing my back, trying to calm me down. I take a deep breath and continue.

"When I close my eyes I can feel the second that the plane is hit. There are six of us on board, my wingman, Dominic, is on the radio with the base. The seconds feel like hours. It's like living your life in a slow-motion hell. I'm the last to eject. For a split second, I don't want to eject. Part of me wants to let the plane crash with me in it so maybe I can be with Shay. But then, I quickly snap out of it, yell at Dom to eject and then I pull the two eject handles under my armrest. I'm responsible for the lives of my crew and I can't leave them stranded behind enemy lines. I need to save them, just like they would save me. When the plane hits, the heat is intense and the smell is putrid. I quickly find my crew, everyone except Dom. We are all pretty banged up: broken bones, cuts, and burns. I'm a mangled mess, but I have to find Dom. He's my responsibility, my family, all I have left in the world. No one ever gets left behind. We didn't land that far from the crash site. I have them stay put, taking care of their injuries while I look for Dominic. The plan was I would find Dom, bring him back to the group and then figure out how to get the hell out of there. As I get closer to the crash site, the smoke is burning my eyes and lungs. Then I hear the cries of the children, and my heart breaks. I get to Dom, detach him from his shoot and drag him away from the plane. There is so much chaos that no one paying any attention to me, that is until a little boy comes up to me, begging for help. I know I've got burns everywhere and at least one leg is broken, but I can't let these people die. I go back again and drag some children away from the thick black smoke. There was another explosion, my back was toward the plane. Dominic and I were both hit with shrapnel, me in my back and legs. Dom was hit in his chest. I should have pulled him further away. I should have done my job better. Maybe if I did, no one would have died. Everything is a little foggy after that. The next thing I know, I'm in a hospital bed. Dominic didn't make it, and I was given a medal I didn't want. All I wanted was my best friend to be alive, not some medal."

She's rubbing my back, trying to sooth me, but my body is shaking and I can't seem to stop it.

"Do you want to stop?"

"It won't change anything."

"So, when you said the subway was a trigger for you, it was the smell and the sound of the metal screeching that reminded you of the crash and the aftermath?"

"Yes, it was everywhere. The little kids were crying and begging for help. I tried. I really tried, but I couldn't help them. Hell, I couldn't even save Dominic. I'll take that guilt to my grave."

"You can't blame yourself for all of this. You did nothing wrong. If anything, you did everything you could to help. Don't condemn yourself to hell because of it. I think we should stop for today and then tomorrow we can go back further to Shay."

"Maybe you're right, maybe I need a break."

"There's a little cafe a few blocks down that makes some great soups. Do you want to come with me?"

"Sure, but no more talk about the past."

"You've got a deal. You can help me grade papers."

I laugh. "Don't tell me they are in your bag of tricks."

"Why do you think teachers carry huge bags? I'm more prepared than any survivalist."

We're both laughing as we begin to walk. The change of scenery will do me good. When we reach the restaurant,

I'm surprised, it's nothing like I was expecting. The place is a little quirky café. We order our food and take a seat in the back. "I would have never found this place on my own. It's really off the beaten path."

"I know. I found it when I first moved here. In the beginning, I got lost so much, but it was a blessing. That's how I found so many of my favorite places." She's twisting the paper from her straw into a little windmill. "Mick, I've been thinking about something all day. I want you to hear me out before you say no," she says just as the waitress comes with our soup and grilled cheese sandwiches.

"Okay, I'm listening."

"I know were weren't going to talk about the past for the rest of the night, but I just want to throw this out there. I think you need to take a trip to Covington. You need to get closure and you're not going to get it until you address the roadblock in your past. Maybe talking to Shay's family would help you find that closure. Maybe when you went before, it was still raw for them. Maybe now they will be willing to see you. You don't have to go it alone; I will go with you. When you go to your next appointment, you can mention it to your doctor, see what he thinks."

I'm staring at her in disbelief. How could someone I hardly know want to do so much for me? "Why would you do that for me? You hardly know me." Her cheeks become flushed and her eyes are darker than usual.

"Mick Callan, how could you even say that to me? I think it's safe to say that we are beyond a hello/goodbye relationship on a New York City bench. I mean, Jesus, I even told you about my father. That's something I don't share very easily."

"Wow, I really pissed you off, sorry."

"Forgiven, we are friends and we will always be friends and the sooner you accept that, the better off we will all be. Now back to my question, what do you think?"

"Let me think about it, fair?"

"Fair, but don't wait too long. Before we know it, winter will be here and the weather will be crazy. Oh, my friend, Jackie, just came in; I want you to meet her. I'll be right back."

Before I can say anything, she's out of the chair and heading toward the front door. I'm not really in the mood for company but she has a way of always making me say yes even when I want to say no.

"Mick, this is Jackie."

I get up and pull out the chair for her. "Nice to meet you. Please, join us." She's younger than I was expecting and stunning.

"Thank you. I can't stay long. I was on my way home to grade papers and realized I forgot to eat lunch today. I figured I better stop now or it would be cold cereal tonight."

"You're welcome to stay here. Raven has roped me into helping her grade papers, what's a few more?"

"I would love the help but I have to get home. My parents are in Switzerland and once a week I Skype with them."

"Is Switzerland where you grew up?"

"Yes. I know, I'm a long way from home. Having Raven here helps."

The pager in her hand lights up and makes the oddest buzzing sound. "Oh my order is ready; I've got to run. I'll see you at school tomorrow. Mick, it was a pleasure to finally meet you."

Just like a whirlwind, she's gone. "Wow, she breezed in and out in a flash."

"Yeah, she's like that. We better get started on these papers."

She passes me half the stack, an answer key, and a red pen. "What subject is this?"

"Social Studies. They have to name all the National Holidays and they have to identify historic places, like the White House, Lincoln Memorial, and the Statue of Liberty. Just follow the answer key and you should be fine. If anyone gets a hundred percent, you have to put a couple of stars and write something positive."

We sit, silently grading the papers and I'm amazed at some of the answers the kids are giving, even the wrong ones are kind of funny. It's hard not to give them credit for their sense of humor.

"Okay, I have a total of three that got a perfect score. This one kid even drew some pictures to go along with his answers. He's really talented." I pass her the papers and she's smiling.

"Yeah, that's Michael. He's very smart; I swear that boy can sell ice to an Eskimo. I think he'll go far in life."

"Do you ever wonder what happens to the children you teach?"

"All the time. Sometimes I find it hard not to want to keep them with me forever. It is a fine line between teaching and mothering. That balance can be difficult. I can only hope that I've made some sort of impression on them that they will carry with them the rest of their lives."

She quietly finishes packing up her stuff while I clear the table. She seems lost in her own thoughts but I don't pry. "I'm going to go back to the mission tonight. Do you want to share a cab?"

"Actually I'm not that far from here, I thought I would walk."

"I'll walk you home. There's no reason for you to be walking alone."

"Mick, you don't have to do that. I can take care of myself."

"Humor me, Raven. Let me act like a big brother and walk you home—please." I'm sure I sound desperate but for some reason I feel like something is off. What that something is I've no clue.

"Well, I don't have a brother, but, if you insist." She stifles a yawn, passes me her bag with all the books in it, and we head out.

Chapter Ten

The walk to Raven's place was not bad and this time I was able to hail a cab pretty quick. When I get to the mission, I'm just in time for the last sermon of the night. Once again, Pastor Clarence hits a home run with his message. I quickly help clean up and head into the kitchen where I know I will be able to talk to him alone.

"I was hoping you were going to come back here tonight. You were on my mind all day. If you don't mind me asking, how was your appointment today?"

I pour us each an ice-cold glass of milk for dunking and try to formulate my words. I know I need to talk to him about this but I also don't want to trigger anything for him.

"It was good and bad. It was good that I feel like I have some sort of hope. However, getting to the point where I might be able to function is not going to be easy. I'm a grown man with a lot of homework. I have to write an impact statement. Then, I'm supposed to journal all my thoughts leading up to what I think my triggers are. It's not just one thing for me; I lost my wife, which is a major trigger, and then my plane crashed, killing so many innocent people, including my best friend." My stomach is in knots and his silence is not helping me. I look at him and his eyes are closed.

After a beat, he opens them and looks at me. "So, what is the purpose of having you relive the events?"

"It's a type of treatment for PTSD. There are four steps and confronting the demons is one of them. Maybe if I can confront them and believe that my choices were not what brought them on, maybe that might finally help me live with myself." I hear myself and I don't sound very convincing so how can I expect him to believe me.

He stops his cookie in mid-air and raises his eyebrows as if to say, *"Do you hear what you sound like?"* "What did your friend say about all of this?"

"She is such a positive person. Honestly, I've never met anyone like her before. She has so much faith and I'm not talking just spiritual. She honestly believes that good will always win."

"She sounds amazing. I would love to meet her when you're ready."

"I would like that, but for now, I think one day at a time is enough for me."

"As long as you keep moving forward and continue to make progress, then I will help you anyway I can."

"Thank you, sir."

After we finish our cookies, I quickly help him clean up

and head to my room in the back of the mission. I put the finishing touches on the counter and now it's ready for the volunteers to stock the shelves. I decide to take a long hot shower while I wait for my meds to kick in. Part of me is hoping I see Shay tonight and yet part of me wants to just sleep. Maybe my need for a normal life might be enough? Maybe if I keep feeding myself that line of bullshit, I just might believe it.

When I finish up I head into bed and think about the day. Could I really do a road trip with Raven? Why would she even want to? Would going back really give me closure? This is all wishful thinking. I could never sleep anywhere near her. What if I have an episode? What if I hurt her? I would never be able to live with myself. She always has such a positive outlook on everything, yet I know there is so much that she hasn't shared with me. Maybe in time I can be for her what she is for me: a true friend beyond any of my wildest expectations. I feel myself drifting off.

The smell of the sea is overpowering. I feel the heat on my face. Not the heat from my crash, this feels warm and soothing.

"Mick, are you going to lay around here all day? My uncle said since we have no school today, we can take his boat out."

When I open my eyes, Jacob is standing there trying to block the sun out of my face. I know this isn't real, I'm either reliving a memory or hallucinating, not sure which. At least it's a good one, a time in my life when I was happy. He offers me his hand and pulls me up off the sand. "Jacob, all you ever want to do is take to the sea. Eventually, you will have to stay on land."

"Well, I've got news for you—I joined the Coast Guard. I'm going in right after graduation."

"I'm not surprised that you joined but I thought you would try and get some college classes under your belt first." We head down toward the dock and climb onto the boat. He's usually very matter-of-fact about everything, yet today, he is hesitating.

"I know that's what Wendy and my parents wanted, but I can't stay away from the sea. My life is here, Mick, just like yours is up there." He points up to the sky as he starts the engine.

"I get it, I really do. But what about Wendy? How does she really feel about it?"

"She gave me an ultimatum: if I join, she walks. I love her, but if she can't support my decision for the future then she really doesn't love me like she should."

"Whatever your decision, you know I will back you all the way."

We quietly head out to our favorite fishing spot. He says he's okay with it but I know better. I know he wanted a future with Wendy but he needs her support not ultimatums.

"Did you pick up the ring for Shay?"

He's good at deflecting the subject. "Yeah, and I was able to get the reservation at that mansion that she loves. I decided to propose to her there."

"You're lucky she supports your decision for the future. I don't think Wendy could see past me being away. Not everyone is cut out for military life. If I don't live my dream, then I will just be chasing what ifs. Life is hard enough without

having to do that."

"I want to be at your swearing-in ceremony, just let me know when and where."

"I know you believe in what I'm doing; thanks for always supporting me."

"Hey, no matter where life takes us, I promise we'll always have a pole and a beer, now shut the fuck up and fish."

He laughs and I close my eyes to enjoy the sun while the boat rocks back and forth. I hear soft music playing and when I open my eyes, I'm no longer with Jacob; I'm with Shay by the fountain. My God, she's so beautiful. I put my hand in my pocket and feel for the ring. If I rub it anymore, I'll rub the felt right off the box.

I clear my throat and try to steady my nerves before I begin. "Shay, I've loved you since the first day I saw you at the farmer's market. I can't imagine my life without you in it. I want to begin and end all of my days with you. With all my heart, I promise to love you and keep you safe. I want to give you the world, and support you in your career. I've already given you my heart, now I want to give you my name." I pull the box out of my pocket, open it up, and drop to one knee.

"Shay Davenport, will you marry me?"

She drops to her knees and places her trembling hands on both sides of my face. "I would be honored to be your wife."

I take her hand and slide the ring on. She's kissing me with those lips, sweeter than blueberries. All I want now is to take her to our room and finally make love to her. I lift her up in my arms and . . .

I hear a loud buzzing and when I open my eyes, I'm at the mission. My alarm has gone off and I'm back to reality.

The past is gone, along with everyone in it. I haven't spoken to Jacob since Shay died. Eventually, I will have to make contact. Maybe if I ever get to the point where I don't blame myself for everything, I'll call him.

I get ready and head out to my bench, making sure I stop at the ATM to get more cash. I'm early, so I head into Starbucks and pick up our order. By the time I leave, she's just rounding the corner. "Good Morning. I was early so I thought I would get breakfast for a change."

We head across the street and settle on the bench. "Did you get everything finished up last night?"

"Yeah, all the papers are graded and I started putting together packets for their winter break. What did you do last night?"

"I went back to the mission and talked with Pastor Clarence for a bit. I had another dream, hallucination or whatever the heck they are. This time I was fishing with my best friend, Jacob."

"When was the last time you spoke to him?"

"When I went back for Shay's funeral. He's in the Coast Guard. I'm not really sure where he's at now," I add. She's picking at her breakfast sandwich, not looking at me. "Hey, are you okay?"

"It makes me sad to think you have friends but you're too scared to face them. You did nothing wrong, but you need to come to that realization on your own. I only hope that you will not disappear on me like you have on them."

I let her words sink in. I know they are not said out of malice, but they still sting all the same. "Raven, I know our friendship is new and you came into this at my worst.

You're seeing me through some pretty awful stuff and you haven't run for the hills. I promise you, I won't be running away, either. I'll be here for as long as you'll let me."

She reaches in her bag of tricks, pulls out a notebook and passes it to me. "In there you'll find all the notes from yesterday and I put the beginning of your impact statement on a separate piece of paper. I think you should review it all to make sure I haven't missed anything. We should meet at school later and we can work on the rest of your homework."

"Okay. Come on, I'll walk you to school. If we don't leave now, you'll be late." I toss out the trash and we head toward the school. I leave her with the promise that I will be sitting on the bench outside of her school when she is done with work.

Chapter Eleven

After leaving Raven safely at school, I decide to head up to Central Park. There are a lot of little ins and outs of that park that I could lose myself in. I stop by the Park Information Center and get a map. There are so many different points of interest but the one that really catches my eye is the Alice in Wonderland statue. Lately, I feel like I've fallen through a rabbit hole and landed between a world of the living and the dead.

I follow the map and I'm surprised to learn the park is over eight-hundred acres. There are also thirty-six bridges and no two are alike. The statue is amazing. It was designed so children can climb all over it. It is surrounded by park benches, then grassy fields and trails. The leaves are turning, and I find a spot under a tree. I pull out the notebook and begin reading what Raven wrote. I notice that she added some questions.

I know the purpose of this homework is to be really honest with myself, however, facing the truth is not always easy. Sometimes that truth can take you on a very dark path. I need to address each one of her questions before I move on to Shay.

"Did you think if you stood on the plane that you could have steered it away from the people or was it to be with Shay?"

I honestly think it was to be with Shay. I knew I wouldn't be able to control the plane.

"Why do you feel guilty for Dominic's death? You pulled him from the plane, how were you to know that it wasn't far enough?"

I feel guilty about Dom's death because. I should have dragged him further from the wreckage, I was trained to know better. Instead, I was more worried about helping others.

"If you would have taken the time to pull him further away and other people would have died, would you feel responsible for them?"

Yes, of course I would. After all, it was my plane that crashed into their village. I take responsibility for all of it.

"When did everyone become your responsibility?"

The day I lost Shay. I wasn't there to save her but maybe I could save someone else. If I can, then maybe I can stop someone from living in my daily hell.

I flip the book over and work my way forward from the back pages. I don't even know where to begin with Shay's story. I take a deep breath and find the courage to begin putting it all down on paper.

Shay Davenport

I made promises to her that I didn't keep. I promised I would keep her safe and support her career choices. I promised her family that I would always put Shay first. Promises made with the best intentions but still, they were broken.

Shay always talked her cases through with me. Sometimes it takes an outsider to look at a situation and see where all the cracks are. We talked about her last case. The family was in trouble, on the verge of falling apart. The husband had just gotten back from Afghanistan. He was in a dark place. Why didn't I see how unsafe the situation was? I encouraged her to go with her gut and put her feelings aside. Was I wrong? Did she go with her heart and not her gut? I'll never know and that's my biggest obstacle. She's dead, and all I have are unanswered questions.

We were only married a month when my Captain broke the news to me. At first, I didn't believe him. I tried calling her family; no one would take my calls. When I finally got a hold of Jacob, he told me in detail what happened. Shay had gotten close to the boy she was counseling, a little too close. She knew it was against the rules, but she gave him her cell number and told him if he was scared or just needed to talk, he could call her. Apparently, when the trouble started at this boy's home, he didn't call the police; he called Shay. She got there, saw that the situation was escalating and called the police. By the time they arrived, she had already worked her way inside and made herself a barrier between the boy and his father. The man shot his wife, Shay, and his son. Then, he turned the gun on himself. Within minutes, everyone was dead.

Jacob was able to get emergency leave and was waiting for me when I arrived back to Covington. He met me at the train station with a look on his face that told me there was more.

"Mick, Shay's parents already buried her."

"Why would they do that? They never let me say good-bye. I'm her husband, what gave them the right to do this without me?"

"You know what a small town this is. I don't have the answers but if we go to the farm, maybe one of her brothers will talk to us."

Jacob took me to the farm to see them. I needed answers. Only Madison, her oldest brother, agreed to see me. I was always closest to him so I'm not surprised he was the one willing to talk to me.

"Why, Madison? Why didn't they wait for me? They knew I was on my way home. Why?"

"Because they blame you, Mick. They felt that you filled her head with fantasies. You made her believe that she was making a difference in the world. That she was saving children and helping to put families back together, but, in the end, there was no one there to save her. You promised that you would always put her before you, that you would keep her safe. You weren't around, and my sister is dead. I'm not saying they are right, I'm just telling you how they feel."

"That's crazy. How could they believe such a thing? She was happy. She was doing what she always wanted to do. Surely they saw that. I'm her husband; how could they just cut me out?"

"Look, Mick, they need someone to blame. They're trying

to work through their grief and, if that's what it's going to take, then let them have that. You know the truth; you'll always know that in her heart Shay was saving children and putting families back together again. That's what really matters. Now I think it's best if you don't come back here, again. You're a constant reminder to them—to all of us—of what we lost." He turned and walked away, leaving Jacob and me standing in disbelief. That's the last time I saw or heard from her family.

I don't know how long I was standing there in shock until Jacob finally pulled me towards the car. Who knows, maybe they are right. Maybe if I wasn't deployed, I would have been there to stop her from going into that house. Every one I've ever loved is gone—my parents, Dominic, and Shay. Maybe it really is *my fault. Like a black cloud of doom following me.*

Jacob took me to the cemetery. I just sat there. I couldn't feel anything except an empty hole in my soul. I couldn't even shed a tear. what kind of monster does that make me? Perhaps I need to back away from Raven? Part of me thinks I should but the other part of me is selfish and, God help me, I really need her friendship right now. I know that she's always giving and I'm always taking. All I can hope for is to be at a point when the scales finally balance.

I look at my watch and I realize I'll never make it in time to meet Raven. I don't want her to worry; I'll send her a text.

Me: Hey, I've been doing my homework and I got lost with time. I won't make it to meet you.

Raven: I can wait for you.

Me: Maybe you shouldn't. I'm not really in a good place. I can meet you tomorrow after my appointment.

Raven: All the more reason we should meet tonight. You know I'm not going to take no for an answer, so you should just meet me.

Me: You're a very stubborn woman. I don't know that I can be around crowds right now.

Raven: My roommate is gone for a few days, so why don't you come to my place. Don't worry, I won't cook. I'll pick up Chinese food for us. Say around six?

Me: Are you sure?

Raven: I'll see you at six.

Me: Stubborn woman.

Raven: Get used to it.

She's seen me through everything up until now; I can't walk away. I go back to my homework. Writing down every feeling and emotion. I know I have to be very open about everything.

Maybe my parents' death was the start of this hell. In some way, I always felt responsible for their death. They were on their way to my soccer game when their car was hit by a drunk driver. Aunt Beth brought me to a grief counselor who said it was not my fault. Hell, my head knew that but my heart told me something different. At thirteen year's old, I blamed myself. After all, if they weren't coming to my game, they never would have been on that road. Maybe there is some sort of black cloud hanging over me.

Back to Shay. My faith tells me that she is in a good place. How could she be? —she's not with me.

I stare at the scribble on the pages and realize I need to get going. I'm not sure If I'm going to show this to Raven. What would she think of me?

Chapter Twelve

I get to Raven's house and stand outside. The tug of war in my head is killing me. I need her friendship and compassion but I don't need her to see me like this; so broken and tortured. I'm about to walk away, when the door opens and she steps out.

"I thought you might have a hard time after today. We don't have to talk but at least come in for a hot meal." She's standing at the top of the steps with one hand on her hip and the other holding the door open. "Mick, I'm not taking no for an answer and the food is getting cold."

I head up the stairs all the time mumbling how stubborn she is.

"It's not the biggest two bedroom but, by Manhattan standards, this is a palace. I figured we could eat in the living room."

I have a seat on the sofa and I swear she must have

ordered enough food for an army!

"I didn't know what you liked so I ordered a few different things. Besides, you know with Chinese food, an hour after you eat it, you're hungry again."

"You're not kidding; it looks like you ordered everything on the menu." I haven't eaten all day and everything smells amazing.

"I love Chinese food, especially the next day. And let's not forget the fortune cookies. So, besides your homework, what did you do today?"

I like the way she slides that right in there. "I went to explore Central Park again. I didn't realize how big it actually is. Today I discovered the Alice in Wonderland statue."

"Oh, that statue is amazing. When you get real close to it, you can see where all the kids hands have worn the patina off."

She passes me another container of food. I have no clue what I'm eating but it is fantastic. "I like to run, but Jackie runs marathons and sometimes we run together through Central Park. I like the different scenery and the wide variety of people. Some of the trails make you forget you're in a big city."

"Jackie seems very nice. In a city this big, I'm glad you have each other."

"Yeah, we're more like sisters. She's a little bit younger than me, so I'm always watching out for her."

I'm so full, I don't think I could eat another bite. I push my plate away and lean back. "Raven, I don't think you realize it but you have a very mothering way about you, and I mean that in a good way."

"Sometimes I don't even realize I'm doing it."

"That's what makes it genuine. It's never forced or thrown on anyone. You really do care." I pass her my journal and take a deep breath. "I also wrote the impact statement. I kept it short and simple. Well, as simple as it could be considering what I was writing."

She looks down at the journal and then back up at me. "I thought we weren't going to talk about this tonight."

"I can't keep hiding from it. I'll clean up while you read."

She curls into the sofa and is soon absorbed in the journal. I notice whenever she's nervous she tugs at her ear. She's tugged at it so much that it's red. I hear a few gasps and I see a few tears but then I see her cheeks get red and I know she got to the end. She finally closes the journal and puts it down in front of me.

"Mick, I know our friendship might seem a little bit unconventional to someone on the outside looking in, but I don't give a fuck what anyone thinks. You might feel that you're the taker in this friendship, but you don't realize how much you're actually giving. You're the first person that I've been able to open up to, outside of Marco and Jackie, about anything personal. We were brought into each other's life for a reason. I'm a lot tougher than you think and I'm not going anywhere."

"You have to promise me something. If it ever gets to be too much, you'll walk away."

"I can't do that. It's just not in my genes. I learned a long time ago that you can't turn back the hands of time. No matter what happens in life, I have faith and that keeps me moving forward."

I pick up the journal and quickly put it in my backpack. "My appointment is early in the morning, so I will not be able to meet you for coffee. I'm also going to talk to the doctor about making the trip to Covington. I didn't forget your offer; I wanted to see what he thinks."

"Will you call or text me to let me know how you are?"

"I promise I will."

"Are you going back to the mission tonight?"

"Yeah, I built a retail space so they can sell some of the donations and I want to make sure everything went okay when they stocked the shelves today."

"Wow, so you can do other things besides flying. Maybe you can work as a carpenter or something like that."

"One day at a time. First, I need to get to the point where I feel comfortable enough to live in an apartment."

She tries to stifle a yawn and I know it's getting late. "I better get back to the mission before it gets any later. I promise I'll let you know how it goes," I reiterate. She gets up and walks me to the door. She's looking down and picking imaginary lint off her pants. "What's the matter, Raven?"

"I really want this to work for you, but I also worry that once you've got a handle on it, you'll move on. It's selfish, I know, but I have no siblings and I all I can hope for is that you'll always remain part of my life."

I take both her hands in mine and squeeze. "Look at me, Raven. Neither one of us has any family, so we've become a family by choice. Sometimes that's better than blood. I promise you—right here, right now—that I will never disappear on you." I give her a hug and head out.

It was easy to hail a cab from her place. I want to get to the mission before Pastor Clarence calls it a night. I get there just as he's closing up for the evening. I quickly begin helping him organize the sanctuary for the morning service. When I'm done, I look over toward him, and he's conversing with two men. I tilt my head toward the kitchen and he nods. I head into the kitchen and wait for him.

He comes in, shuffling his feet, and laughs when he sees I have the cookies and milk waiting for him. "I gather you want to talk to me. You know, you don't have to bribe me with cookies and milk?"

"I know, but I look forward to our little routine at night."

"So, what's on your mind?"

"I have an appointment tomorrow with the doctor. The first step was to write down everything that I think might be a trigger for me."

"Did you finish?"

"I think so. I think there are things that happen to us in life that shape us and give us courage but I wouldn't say they are a trigger for me."

"Such as?"

"My parents died when I was thirteen and I had to move from Nebraska to Louisiana to live with my aunt. My aunt put me into grief counseling at our church and they taught me how to cope with my anxiety. I'm feeling doubtful that I will be able to come back from everything. Don't get me wrong; I want to, but I can't see that light at the end of the tunnel."

"There's always a light, Mick. Sometimes we need to get

the fog out of the way to see it. What did your friend say about all this?"

"She is always so positive. She believes I will get better, that I will find a way to cope. She's not one to look back."

"Well, I think you should follow her lead. She can probably see past the fog that you seem to be trapped in." He closes the cookies and pushes them away, knowing that neither one of us needs any more. "The best advice I can give you is don't tell the doctor what you think he wants to hear. Tell him the God's honest truth. That's the only way you're going to get to the other side of this." He gets up squeezes my shoulder before heading out. I clean up and then hit the showers. I'm too anxious to sleep, so I stock some of the higher up shelves. Hopefully staying busy will keep my mind off of tomorrow. It's one thing to tell Raven what happened—she's my friend—but to tell a total stranger . . . it might be impossible.

I'm finally starting to feel tired. I climb into my cot and begin my meditation. Before long, I drift off to sleep.

Chapter Thirteen

I'm up before my alarm (not that I really slept much) but at least there were no nightmares, hallucinations, flashbacks or whatever the fuck they are. To say I'm nervous about today is an understatement. First things first, I need to get ready and then go help with breakfast.

Time moves quickly when I stay busy, but today it seems like it's dragging. I finally clean up and head out to my appointment. The closer I get to the building, the more anxiety I'm feeling. My gut is twisting into knots and my heart is racing. I have to stay strong. I stand outside for a good ten minutes. I look down and realize I'm standing on top of the subway grate. Before I can move, I hear that metal on metal noise, the brakes grinding to a halt. The smell is putrid. I feel the sweat beading up on the back of my neck. I close my eyes and try to fight the fear, fight the bile rising in my throat.

"Step inside dumb ass."

My eyes fly open and look around for him. I don't know why I expect to see him here. I know Dom is dead but, for a split second, I could swear I felt him push me toward the door. I mumble under my breath as I open it and step inside. "Maybe you're the dumb ass for dying."

I find the nearest men's room and clean up before heading in for my appointment. Of course I'm given another load of papers to fill out. I thought the government was trying to make all records electronic, doesn't look like they got very far with that. I don't have to wait long before I'm taken back. When I step inside the room, Dr. Joe Finley introduces himself. The room is set up like a living room and I take a seat across from Dr. Doogie Howser, all the while trying not to laugh. He looks like he just graduated high school.

"So, Doc, how does this work?"

"Did you do your impact statement?"

I reach in my backpack about to pull out my impact statement, but I stop in midstream. I'm leery about giving it to him. "Yeah, but I've got a couple of questions."

He puts his pen down, looks up at me, and puts his fingers together in the shape of a steeple. He keeps tapping his index fingers together, and for some reason, I find that very annoying. "Are you really the doctor or is this some sort of test?"

"You're not the first person to ask that question. I've been blessed with my mother's genes. They all look very young and live a long life. I can assure you I'm old enough to be your doctor."

He puts his hand out and I give him my impact statement, keeping my journal in my backpack. "So how does this work?"

"First, I need to get to know you and get a better understanding of the events in your life that have brought you here. That's what your impact statement is for. The details of the events usually come out when I have you read me your journal. Sometimes the journal is more for you than for me. It depends how open you are going to be with me. I'm not here to judge you, Mick. I'm just here to help, if you let me.

Now, I know that you had three major events in your life. Your parents died when you were thirteen. Your wife died while you were deployed. And finally, your plane was shot down, killing your best friend and some local residents."

"You make it sound so cut and dry."

"On the contrary, I read your file and I'm amazed you kept it together for so long. Tell me about your parents' car accident."

"What's there to tell? I mean, they were in an accident and died instantly. After that, I went to live with my aunt in Covington, Louisiana."

"Did you have any type of grief counseling?"

"Yes, my aunt made sure I had everything I needed. Is this really necessary?" I feel myself getting more and more agitated.

"Mick, you can't speed through the events in your life. Sometimes you have to look back on them for guidance. Every minute of your past made you who you are today.

You put these events on your impact statement so they must be major for you. Why are you here and what do you expect to get out of all of this?"

He places the statement face down on his notepad and waits for me to answer him. "I want to be fixed."

"Exactly what does fixed mean to you?"

He air quotes the word fixed and I try not to lose my cool. "Oh, I don't know, maybe being able to sleep indoors, like a normal person, and not live on a park bench would be a good start. Maybe waking up and knowing my hands won't be around anyone's throat. Hell, I can't even walk into the subway station. I want a normal life, Doc. I feel like I fought hard to stay alive, even when I didn't want to; my body had other ideas. I feel responsible for everything that has happened and I don't know how to shut that off. I feel like I'm in one huge fucking pity party!"

"Mick, you didn't cause your parents' car accident. You weren't responsible for your wife's death, and you weren't responsible for your plane being shot down. Tell me why you feel responsible?"

"I know in my mind I'm not responsible, but my heart is telling me otherwise. How do I shut that off?"

"It will take time. You're not responsible for your parents' accident. You couldn't predict that a drunk driver would hit them. What makes you think you're responsible for your wife's death? You couldn't have stopped it even if you were in the country."

I explain to him why her family holds me responsible. How insistent they were on her not going to college and pursuing her dreams.

"Is that what Shay wanted?"

"No, she wanted to help put families back together. Her parents never got it, they thought it was a pipe dream."

"Did they tell you this or are you assuming this?"

Wow, his tone and the look on his face tells me he's not about to pull any punches. "When I got back, they had already buried her. I went to the farm to talk to them and they sent their oldest son Madison to deal with me. He said they blame me."

"Did he say why?"

"When we got engaged, I promised them I would always keep her safe. I would put her before me. They felt her death proved their point, which is the outside world, and everyone in it, is on a downward spiral. The only safe place was with them."

"I'm sure you talked to Shay about her career choice. What she was doing and where she wanted to end up. Was she ever on the fence about any of it?"

"Shay's biggest problem was knowing when to let go. She always had a hard time when a child was either sent back to their family or put in foster care. I always teased her that our house will be filled with puppies and babies. Look, Doc, no job is perfect, we all have those days when we question why we are doing what we're doing. That's when you have to look at the big picture." Now I wonder who is counseling who.

"That's my point, Mick. We all have doubts. Tell me . . . why do you feel responsible for your plane crash?"

"Pretty smooth segue way into my plane crash. I don't feel responsible for the crash itself, but I feel responsible for Dominic's death. I didn't pull him far enough from the plane. I was busy helping the other people. Then there was another explosion; Dom got hit in the chest. If I would have followed protocol, I would have pulled him far enough away. I would have gotten him back to the rest of the crew. He wouldn't have died." I barely get the words out before I feel like I've been punched in the gut. He passes me a box of tissues and waits for me to somewhat get my act together.

"Mick, I think we went over a lot today. Let's break it down by events in your life. At your next appointment, I would like to go deeper into the plane crash."

"Why? Why are you focusing on that?"

"The first two events were out of your control. You weren't even there for both of them. The plane crash is different and I believe that's your biggest obstacle."

"My friend suggested that I should go back home and try to get closure. Do you think, now that so much time has passed, Shay's family would be willing to talk to me."

"There's no guarantee that they will be in a different place emotionally then they were before. Let's put that on the back burner for now and focus on our plan. Monday at ten." He's not asking, he's telling me. If I want this to work, then I have to go along with the plan. I get up and thank him (for what, I don't know) and head out the door.

Chapter Fourteen

My first appointment was a lot longer than an hour. When I step out on to the street, it's the beginning of rush hour. The intensity of this city is not for the faint of heart. I hail a cab and as I'm heading back to the mission, I shoot a text to Raven.

> Me: Hey, I just got done. I'm okay but heading to the mission.
>
> Raven: Do you want to meet for coffee tomorrow?
>
> Me: Take the weekend and have some fun. I've got more homework to do for Monday's session.
> Raven: Are you blowing me off?

Me: Never, the doctor wants to dig deeper into the plane crash. I need to prepare myself for that. I promise if I need you I will call you.

Raven: Okay, but can you check in by text and let me know how you're doing?

Me: Yes, Mom. Lol

I'm just in time to help serve dinner. I jump in Pastor Clarence's spot so he is freed up to talk to the people as they come through the line. Some days it's the same faces and other days they're all new. Either way, they are people in need. Everyone can get a meal. They are not required to stay for Pastor Clarence's sermon. However, he has a way of making you want to stay and hear him. After dinner, everyone heads into the Sanctuary. It's a full house again. Tonight, he's talking about taking responsibility for yourself. Life might have dealt you a bad hand but it doesn't mean you have to fold. It doesn't entitle you to a hand out. If you only have it in you to be responsible for one person, then be responsible for yourself. Be accountable for your actions good or bad.

When the service is over, I hang back and watch him interact with some of the people. He helps in so many ways. Sometimes, when all else fails, he stops and listens. Sometimes knowing that someone is not judging you, only listening to what is really important to you makes all the difference in the world. I'm very blessed to have two people in my life that care and want to help me.

I head into the kitchen and set up our cookies and milk. It's the little things in my life right now that are bringing me comfort. When Pastor Clarence comes in, he's moving a little bit slower than usual. I've been so focused on me and my problems that, until now, I didn't even notice how tired he looks. "Sir, you look very tired, are you feeling okay?"

"Today was a difficult day. I was notified that one of my military brothers has been placed in Hospice care. He was exposed to Agent Orange and developed cancer."

"I'm so sorry, is there anything I can do for you?"

"Thank you, just keep him in your prayers. I went to see him and he's ready. It's been a long, hard road. Enough about me; what happened at your appointment today?"

I pass him the cookies and take a minute to gather my thoughts. "Well, it was a lot harder than I thought it was going to be. He wants me back in his office on Monday morning. He wants to get into the details of the crash."

"Are you prepared for that?"

"I don't feel like I have much of a choice at this point. I want a normal life or as close to normal as I can get. I sure don't want to continue on like this." He pushes the cookies back toward me.

"Son, I've seen so much, at this point, I wouldn't even know what normal is. All you can do is try your best. Did you ask him about that road trip you were thinking about?"

"Yeah, he made some good points and wanted to wait until we get past my plane crash. Besides, I'm not sure I want to subject Raven to all of that."

"Raven . . . that's a very pretty name. I hope you will bring her around here one day."

"In time, sir. On a happier note, I finished the store. I'm pleased with the way it came out. I would like to take the spare room that you were storing everything in and make it more organized for the volunteers."

"That would be wonderful. Now I need to step away from the cookies. I was doing so good, until today."

I wrap up the cookies and offer to clean up. I watch him shuffle off to bed. As I clean everything up, I say a prayer, thanking God for putting Pastor Clarence in my life. Too many times we take the people in our lives for granted. My thoughts instantly turn toward Raven. I thank God every day that she reached out to me. The day she showed up with her yoga mat for me, I made a promise right then and there that I would never take our friendship for granted.

After hitting the shower, I head into bed. This has become my nightly ritual, deep cleansing breaths, waiting for the inevitable. Then waking up and realizing nothing has changed, I've lost it all. Tonight, I'm not going down that road. I'm going to be strong—I am strong. I keep telling myself that as I drift off to sleep.

My alarm goes off and I made it through the night. I keep thinking about Raven. I don't want all our time spent together to be spent on my past. I want to have fun and I know just the thing.

Me: Hey I know we weren't getting together until tomorrow but would you like to meet me after church today? I thought of something fun we can do.

Raven: Geez you're up early. Where would you like to meet?

Me: Central Park at the 59th and Park entrance. Is noon good?

Raven: See you there!

I fix my cot and get ready to head out front to help out with breakfast. Plus, I don't want to miss the morning sermon.

Sunday mornings always seem to be the busiest at the mission. New faces and regulars, no one is turned away. I quickly head to the park and when I get there, she's waiting for me.

"I know I'm early but after you texted me I couldn't think of anything else. What do you have planned?" She bouncing from foot to foot like a little kid and I can't help but laugh.

"When I was here the other day, I passed the carousel and the zoo. I thought we could have some fun. We can feed the penguins, ride the carousel, and just take a day off from life. It's totally my treat today. "

"I'm game; lead the way! "

We head into the zoo and work our way around every exhibit. It's a lot bigger than I thought and after a while, we stop and rest on one of the benches. My thoughts wander to Shay and what could have been. "I could sit here and watch the children laughing and playing all day long."

"You sound so sad. There is always a chance you can

make a life for yourself. I know it wouldn't be the same as with Shay but I keep thinking back to the other day when we talked about love. It will be different but it can still be good, just different."

"Only happy thoughts today. Now what does your week look like?" She is very engrossed in her cotton candy and she's really not paying any mind to me. I wave my hand in front of her face. "Hello, are you with me?"

"I'm sorry, I haven't had this since I was a kid. I forgot how much fun it is. This time of year the kids are only thinking about Halloween and Christmas. I have to get them to focus on school work and standardized testing. I try to break it up with different things that are fun, yet informative. This week we are letting the kids bring a parent to school and they can talk about what they do for a living. Kind of showing the kids all the different careers that are available to them. Not everyone is destined to go to college. The world needs blue collar workers and people with trades."

"I would think your school wouldn't have to many blue collar workers."

"There are some. What is sad is that not every parent will participate. They are busy and the children are raised by nannies. I can tell you that no matter where I end up in life, rich or poor, I will raise my children myself. Those first only come around once in life and I don't want to miss it."

"I thought I would have children one day. Now that door is closed."

"Never say never. You don't know what life has in

store for you, none of us do. Now, enough of this; I want to go on the merry-go-round again."

"Well, we better hurry, looks like they are going to be shutting down soon."

We get the last ride in before they close down. We are both exhausted, but I don't want this day to end. "How about we get some coffee before you head home."

"My sugar rush from all that cotton candy I ate has worn off so coffee would be a God send right now."

We leave the park and work our way towards her place. Of course there is a Starbucks along the way. I get the coffee while she finds a table in the back for us.

"Tomorrow is going to be another hard day for you. Are you ready for it?"

"I don't think I'll ever be *ready* but I know living like this is not an option."

"Will I see you tomorrow after your appointment? If you can't, can you just shoot me a text to let me know you're okay?"

She stifles a yawn. I'm used to running on little to no sleep but she needs her rest. "I promise either way I will get in touch with you. I think we should get you home. Let's share a cab."

We head outside and hail a cab. We haven't even gone five blocks and she's nodding off. When we get to her place, I walk her up to her door.

"You know, I'm a big girl and I can get myself home, right?"

"Yeah, I know, but this makes me rest easier. I had a great day today."

"I did, too. Next time, we should try renting one of those boats."

"I would love to. Now go."

I watch her go inside and get back into my cab and head toward the mission.

Chapter Fifteen

Another Monday morning but this one is different. Today I'm headed back to my doctor. I really didn't sleep at all last night. I was tempted to go sleep on my bench but I forced myself to stay inside. Baby steps, that's what I keep telling myself. I get checked in with Dr. Finley and this time, I don't have to wait. This time, he's waiting on me. He reaches out and shakes my hand. Even though he looks like a kid, he has a firm grip.

"How was your weekend?"

"I took a day off of worrying about my life and went with my friend to Central Park. We went to the zoo and rode the carousel. It was nice."

"That's it, just nice? I would think it would be great to just have some fun for a change."

"I thought it would be too, but I was reminded of all I lost with the death of my wife. She died and I lost the hope of ever having a family. I lost what little I had left in the world."

"You don't think that you can have a family someday?"

"No, I don't."

"Well, if you keep trying to duplicate your wife then it's safe to say you'll be stuck right where you are for the rest of your life. Is that what you really want?"

I'm not answering him and he's not budging on this. Finally, I take a deep breath and give in to his stare down. "What do you want me to say?"

"For starters, the truth would be nice. What do you want, Mick? Say it."

I slam my fist on the side table and nearly knock over the lamp, yet he's not startled. "I want to go back damn it. Back before all of this happened. I want a fucking do over and I know it's not possible. So, you tell me Doc, now what!?" I'm on the edge of my seat. My whole body is trembling. I grab a bottle of water and practically down the entire thing while trying to avoid eye contact.

"You have to look past the words and the pain. Look past the loss, and all those memories. Learn to accept that she's gone. You can't do any of that until you let go of the guilt and your unfounded notion that you are responsible for every damn thing that happens in life!"

"How? How the hell am I supposed to do that?"

"By working with me and not against me. I'm not the enemy, Mick. I'm here to help you even if, right now, you hate me. Do you have your journal?"

I reach down and pull it out of my backpack. I pass it to him but he holds up his hand stopping me.

"No, read me what you wrote about your wife."

He puts his pad down and with his arms on his legs, he leans forward.

"Take all the time you need."

I take a deep breath to try and calm my racing heart. "Her name was Shay. I made promises to her that I didn't keep." My fingers tremble and I try not to tear at the pages as I read to him. My throat gets dry and scratchy. The memories of sitting at Shay's graveside flood my mind. Nothing to touch, to say goodbye to—nothing.

I finish and the trembling in my hands is so bad. Then, it finally hits me and the flood gates open. My tears begin to fall, hitting the pages in my journal and the words begin to smudge. Doc reaches over and takes the book out of my hands. He puts a box of tissues in front of me and says nothing. All the unshed tears have picked now to show up. I sit there for at least twenty minutes and let the grief wash over me. When I finally gain some composure, he gets up and takes a seat next to me.

"This was a big step for you. You made a promise to protect her. I'm sure you made that with the best intentions but life doesn't always go the way we want it to."

"The damn ink wasn't even dry on our license. All I'm left with are faded memories and a broken heart."

"You said if you were there maybe you could have stopped her from going into that house. We all have times in our lives we wish we could go back to. We want that because now we're filled with the knowledge of what will happen. We want to stop the bad stuff from ever happening. The reality is, if we could go back, the same thing would happen all over again."

"Is this supposed to make me feel better, cause it's not."

"It's a ladder to healing, one rung at a time. If you went back to that day and you were home with Shay, she gets the call. Walk me through the steps of what you would do."

"That's a stupid question. I would stop her from going."

"She doesn't go because you wouldn't let her. You stopped her from doing the job she loved and was trained to do. The outcome for that family is the same. Now what? What happens to Shay now? What happens to the love and trust you have created between the two of you?"

"It would be destroyed because of my fear." My own words hit me like a sucker punch in the gut.

"If we could all live our life in a bubble what would this world look like? You can't change the outcome. You were not responsible for her murder, the man who pulled the trigger was. If you were here and stopped her, sooner or later you would have broken her spirit. The same way you moved on when your parents died, you need to do that now. One day at a time." He gets up and goes to his desk while I gather my stuff. "I'm giving you a few days off. I want you to spend the time thinking about everything we discussed. I'll see you back here Thursday at two. At that time, we will talk about the crash."

Once again it's a demand and not a choice. "I'll see you then."

When I get outside, I decide to walk for a while. It's a beautiful afternoon and I have no place to be. I'm wandering around the city, taking in the sites when I stumble upon the South Street Seaport. To say it's amazing is an understatement. I love museums and this place has ships set up as museums along with two blocks of galleries, shops, and restaurants. It's closed to automobile traffic, which is nice not having to worry about getting nailed by some of these crazy drivers. After spending hours tooling around, I take a seat on a nearby bench. My thoughts wander to Jacob. All the times we spent on his uncle's boat. I don't know where he is but maybe it's time I find out. The last time I saw Jacob, he was at the foot of my hospital bed, drilling my doctor. He probably didn't realize I could hear everything he was saying. I just remember waking up and requesting no visitors. After that, I never heard from him again. I pull out my phone to text him but find three text messages from Raven. Shit, I forgot I had the phone on silent. As I scroll through them, I'm reminded how much her friendship has helped me.

> **Me: Hey, sorry I missed your messages, my phone was on silent. The session was intense and I've got more homework. I also have appointments with him all week. I'll try to meet up with you for morning coffee, just not sure which day yet. Don't worry I'm okay.**

> **Raven: If you need to talk before then give me a call. Are you sure you're not avoiding me?**

> **Me: Never, I just need some time. I'll check in with you . . . promise.**

Raven: Okay.

I know I'm in a dark place right now and the last thing I want is for her to see me like this, but I'm determined to get above the darkness. I take a deep breath and scroll through my contacts, not that there are so many and find Jacob's number. No time like the present.

Me: I know it's been awhile but I wanted to check in with you.

Jacob: Where the hell are you? Are you okay?

Me: New York City. I'm doing better than before.

Jacob: What the fuck are you doing there?

Me: Trying to get things worked out in my head.

Jacob: Is it working?

Me: Slowly, but yes. Where are you?

Jacob: Maryland, which puts me really close to you. When you're ready we should get together. Just give me a heads up and I can swing time off.

Me: I will. Take care.

Jacob: You too, my friend.

I get up and head toward the mission. Maybe spending more time there will ground me. There is always someone walking through that red door that has a heavier burden then the person before.

Chapter Sixteen

*I*hated to back away from Raven but I need it. I'm sure she would understand. I needed to prepare myself mentally for this appointment with Dr. Finley. I was hoping my late night talks with Pastor Clarence would put my mind at ease. He's good but he's not God. I know in the end that's who I have to answer to.

My bus got me to my appointment a little early and Dr. Finley is waiting for me.

"You came back again, that's a plus."

"Did you really think I wouldn't?"

"Some people, in similar situations, choose not to. Sometimes the fight is too much."

"When I think of these appointments in my mind, I see the scales of justice. One has to balance out the other. I can't expect to come here and everything will turn out like sunshine and roses. Working through the pain is bad, but feeling like I belong is better."

"That's an interesting way to look at it. So, today I want to talk about the crash. Why do you think you didn't pull Dominic far enough away from the plane?"

"Well, he's dead and I'm not, isn't that reason enough?" I know I sound nasty but really, what the fuck kind of question is that?

"He's dead and you think it's your fault. Not the person who shot down your plane? Not the other men for n<u>o</u>t helping you find Dominic? Not the people who were begging you for help? Just you and only you were responsible for Dominic's death?"

"You can try to shift the blame to whomever you want from the President of the United States on down. The truth is, these were my men and, therefore, they were my responsibility." I feel the sweat start building up on the back of my neck.

"I think there is something that you're blocking out. Something that could change everything. Dig deep, Mick. If you don't, then you'll never get past this."

I close my eyes and replay that day in my head just like I've done every day since I woke up in that hospital. "Dom and I were the last to eject."

"Stop right there. Why?"

"For a split second, I didn't want to, but then it hit me that I'm responsible for everyone."

He holds up his hand stopping me again. "I want to know why Dominic didn't eject. Why was he still there when the other men already ejected?"

"I don't know. I yelled at him to eject and I pulled the

two levers under my armrest. He followed suit."

"Do you think he froze?"

"Are you crazy? He was the best co-pilot."

"Haven't you ever wondered why he landed so close to the crash?"

I feel the room beginning to spin and my head is about to explode. "I yelled eject! I kept yelling 'eject damn it, eject!'. I don't know why he waited seconds after me. The only thing I can figure is he knew my mindset. Maybe he thought I wouldn't eject. Maybe he was waiting for that, which just confirms his death is my fault." I grab my bottle of water from the table and down it. My throat is parched and the cold water feels good. When I look over at Dr. Finley, he's flipping through pages.

"Actually, Mick, I think he froze. If he really thought you weren't going to eject, he would have been yelling at you. Instead, you were the one doing the yelling. Face the fact—he froze. It's more common than you think."

That entire horrible day is running through my head like an express train. I replay the last seconds in that plane. "Eject, eject! Now God damn it, now!"

It becomes clearer, he's right—Dom froze. Fuck, why didn't I see this before?

"You're replaying it in your head, what do you see?"

"I'm yelling at him to eject. I pull the levers and he follows. He should have gone before me but he followed me. Even if he did freeze, it doesn't change the fact that I didn't pull him far enough away. It doesn't change the fact that I left him to help others. No matter how you spin it, I still fucked up."

"We could split hairs here all day, but in the end, you're not the Amazing Kreskin. You had no way of knowing that there would even be another explosion, let alone know that it would send shrapnel in your direction. You were given a medal, not for saving yourself, but for saving others. You can accept that or you can wallow in self-pity. The choice is yours."

"How, how do I move forward?"

"By owning it. Could you have done some things differently? Yeah. But, you made split decisions with the information on hand. Hind sight is always twenty-twenty."

I get up and toss my empty water bottle. "When do you want to see me again?"

"Tuesday and Thursday of next week. I want to continue with two days a week."

"Do I have homework?"

"Yes. I want you to look at the positive things in your life. Write them in your journal and we will discuss them on Tuesday. The front desk will make the appointments for you."

"Okay, thank you." I gather my stuff and stop at the front desk before heading out.

I grab a quick bite to eat from a street vendor and head to the mission. When I get there, I find a very long line out the door. I make my way inside and find Pastor Clarence. "What's up with the line?"

"Every fall we pass out winter coats. Our supply this year is short and our line is long."

"What can I do to help?"

He passes me a legal pad. "I've separated the families

from the rest of the group. Can you get their information: sizes they need and any other information that might be important?"

Chapter Seventeen

When I open my eyes and stretch, I'm reminded of how uncomfortable this bench really is. It's early yet, too early for Raven. I head across the street and the baristas are just setting up for the morning rush. After getting cleaned up, I grab a coffee and the paper before going back across the street to wait for her. I keep checking my watch like that will make time go by faster. I'm surprised she's running late today; I know it's a big day for her class. She was worried if the parents were going to show up. I hope they all do. I'm about to text her when I see her rush out of Starbucks and almost knock some guy over. Before I can run across the street to help her, she's already bolting across to me. She pitches me a bottle of water.

"Nice catch, Mick."

She takes off in a full sprint. Even if I ran after her, we wouldn't have time to talk. I pull out my phone and send her a text.

>Me: I know you're busy with the parents today. Can we meet after school to talk?
>
>Raven: Yeah, sorry. I just made it in time. TTYL

I put my phone away and when I look up, the man she nearly plowed down is standing in front of me. His arm outstretched, passing me a bag.

"I figured you might be hungry since the girl that usually buys you breakfast was running late."

I reach out and take the bag. "Thanks; she's a sweetheart."

"What do you know about her?"

I'm trying to figure out what this guy's deal is, but he's giving nothing away. "What's it to you?"

"Well, I could stand here and feed you a line of bullshit."

I hold my hand up cutting him off before he can finish. "Yeah, you could, but that doesn't mean I would tell you anything about her."

"Look, mate, she ran into me this morning . . . as you can tell by my shirt. I just want to know who she is."

I look him up and down and, yeah—he's got money. Expensive suit and watch; it doesn't mean jack to me. "By the looks of you, you can afford to buy another shirt, so, again, what's it to you who she is?"

He offers me his hand. "My name is Jax. She's beautiful and I want to know more."

"Well, Jax, my name is Mick, and yeah, she is beautiful, but more so on the inside. Not very many people will even give me the time of day, let alone buy me breakfast. I'm back from the war and things just aren't right sometimes; she just gets it. She doesn't judge me. What she gives me is more valuable than money—her time. She just gets it. If you want to know more about her, come back tomorrow; she's here every day. That's all you'll get from me, Jax."

I go back to my newspaper, basically cutting off anymore conversation with the guy.

"Okay, Mick. Thanks."

I watch him leave and make a mental note to tell Raven about him later. Right now, I'm going to head back to the South Street Seaport. When I was there yesterday, I purchased a ticket to sail around New York on an 1885 schooner. I think it will do me some good to be out on the water for the afternoon.

The weather was perfect today for my sail around New York. I love history and not being confined to a classroom made it even more fantastic. I picked up a couple of brochures about the other sailing ships they have. Maybe it's something Jacob might want to do. Reaching out to him was a major step for me. Even though that friendship is on hold right now, I know it's one that I don't want to lose. I decided to hang out at the seaport all day and make notes in my journal. With all the different kids here on their field trips, it's very easy to find positive things to write about. I could stare out over the water all day long, but if I don't leave now I will miss Raven.

The pretzel vendor is a block from Raven's school. I grab two of them and some water. I get to her school just as the bell rings. It's always hectic but I don't have to wait too long for her to join me on the bench.

"Hey, sorry about this morning. I was up late getting everything ready for today and I overslept. What happened yesterday?"

"I got you a snack; eat while I talk." I pass her the pretzel and she instantly smiles.

I laugh. "It doesn't take much to make you smile. I went to Dr. Finley, expecting to rehash the crash, instead, we talked about Shay. If I was there and I stopped her from going to help that boy, the outcome would have been worse."

"How so?"

"If I was there I would have stopped her from going. Nothing was going to change the outcome with the family. Eventually, she would have blamed me. In the end, it would have torn us apart."

"What about her family?"

"I feel like I can finally say I did nothing wrong. I loved and supported Shay. I know I promised to keep her safe and I did the best I could but that situation was out of my control. They want to blame me and if that's what helps them heal, then let them. I need to stop worrying about them and worry about my own healing."

"Wow, that's a major step for you."

"It's a major step in the right direction for a change. I'm taking it one day at a time. I went to the South Street Seaport and took a sailing tour of New York. It felt good being out on the water." I take a sip of my water. "I also sent a text message to Jacob."

"Oh, wow! What did he say?"

"He's stationed in Maryland. When I'm ready, he's going to come up to see me. When he does, I would love for you to meet him. It would mean a lot to me."

"Of course, I look forward to meeting him."

"How did the kids make out today?"

"Well, after my coffee mishap, I thought everything was going to be fine. That is until the guy, I nearly plowed over, showed up at school. Apparently, his nephew is in my class."

"Oh, speaking of which, he brought me a sandwich from Starbucks. He was pumping me for information about you," I inform her. Her eyes grow wide and her mouth is hanging open.

"No, he didn't! What the hell? He stayed after class and asked me out. I don't even know him. I told him I was busy and ran out."

"Who is his nephew?"

"Michael, the boy I told you could sell ice to Eskimo's."

"Well the guy seemed nice. Going for coffee is not such a big deal."

She's tugging on her ear which I've come to figure out she does when she's nervous. "What is it, Raven. You might as well just tell me."

"I had a weird feeling when I touched him. I don't know, maybe I'm not ready, yet."

"You know the doc told me that I have to look past the pain and the memories. Maybe you need to do that to move forward. You know, after all, it's just coffee. Talk to Jackie and see what she thinks."

"Maybe . . . I'll think about it. Are you going back to the mission tonight?" she quickly changes the subject. Maybe she really isn't ready, yet. Some things just can't be forced.

"Yeah, I didn't stay there last night. I needed alone time, but I miss my nightly conversations with Pastor Clarence."

"I'm glad you found him and he's helping you."

"I didn't realize how much he's helping me until now. I mean, I know my doctor is trained to do his thing, but sometimes it takes someone who had been through it to really look beyond the obvious and understand the fear that keeps cutting through to the surface."

"Well, when you're ready, I would love to meet him. I need to get going. Do you want to share a cab?"

"Sure," I reply. She quickly hails a cab.

"I'm going to spend the weekend at the Mission. Pastor Clarence has some new projects for me. Besides, I have to work on my homework for next week. Do you have any plans?"

"No, I have papers to grade and I want to catch up on my lesson plans. I'm looking forward to a nice, quiet weekend."

We pull up to her place and I help gather all her stuff and walk her to her door. She gives me a hug and promises to check in with me over the weekend. Weekends without her are the hardest, but I can't monopolize all of her time. She's young and she should have a life. As the cabbie takes me to the mission, I pull out my journal and note all the reasons I'm thankful for my friendship with Raven. I'm determined to get a life, even if I have to master the basics all over again.

Chapter Eighteen

It's Monday morning and I spent the entire weekend helping others. It kind of puts a different perspective on life when you hear someone else's story. I make it to the bench with plenty of time to spare. I notice Jax go inside Starbucks. I look at my watch; if she doesn't get here soon, she will be late for school. I'm about to call her when I see her dart around the corner and quickly duck inside Starbucks. She comes out and heads across the street and hands me a coffee.

"Can I walk with you to school?"

"Of course, is everything okay?"

"Yes, I noticed your friend Jax went inside Starbucks before you came. I don't want to get all 'Big Brother' on you; I just want to make sure you're okay with it."

"I went out with him this weekend. It was very unexpected, but I really enjoyed myself. He seems like a good man, Mick. I just want to take it one day at a time. How was your weekend? Are the nightmares subsiding now that you're in therapy?"

"They are becoming less and less. You know good days and bad days. Some days are better than others. I spent the entire weekend helping others. It really puts things in perspective."

The bell rings and she squeezes my hand. "Let's make today one of those good days." She hugs me before gets up and runs into class. After she gets safely inside I head back to my bench.

When I get there, I find Jax waiting for me. I sit down next to him and he passes me a bag. "I didn't want you to miss a meal on my account."

"Thank you, but I can afford to buy breakfast. It's more about the time I get to spend with Raven."

"How long have you two been friends?"

He seems honestly interested and not just on a fishing expedition. "It's been a couple of months. We met right after I got here. We kind of look out for each other."

"We spent some time together this weekend. She keeps running from me a lot." His stare is intense almost like I have all the answers.

"Well, don't give her a reason to run."

He begins to laugh and I can't help but laugh along with him. "Oh, Mick, if only life were that simple. Is there anything I can do to help your situation?"

As much as he seems to want to genuinely help me, his type of help—I don't need right now. "Thank you, I'm doing okay."

He gets up and tosses his empty cup into the trash. "I've got to get going."

"Jax, don't hurt her," I barely get the words out and he steps back in front of me.

"Never," He growls and with that he's gone.

I head back to the mission. Pastor Clarence is expecting a delivery of coats and I promised him I would help with the distribution. A local radio station did a coat drive and I was not expecting hundreds to be delivered. I'm glad I made it back early to help organize it all. Over the weekend I built floor to ceiling shelving in the room next to the thrift store. I'm at the top of the ladder putting away the last of the coats when there is a knock on the door. I look over my shoulder and it's Chatty Cathy.

"Hey, Cathy, do you need something?"

"It's almost dinner time and I was wondering if you needed help finishing up here?"

"I just finished. I'll wash up and I'll be out in five minutes to help serve," I say. She's not leaving, just standing there staring at me. "Did you need something else from me?"

"I don't want to sound rude, but why are you here? I mean you're nothing like the rest of the people that come through those doors."

"Well, Cathy, has anyone ever told you to *never judge a book by its cover*? What you see on the outside isn't always what's on the inside. Judging people can be hurtful and rude." I stop myself from really tearing into her.

"I'm sorry, I meant no disrespect. I'm just curious as to why you're here. Space is limited and with the nights getting colder, the shelters are bound to fill up fast."

Maybe she's right, maybe I'm taking up a space that might benefit someone else. "Thank you, Cathy, I will keep that in mind. Now, I need to clean up before dinner." I walk past her, not giving her a chance to respond.

Dinner went smoothly and Cathy left right after clean up. Pastor Clarence did his sermon a little differently tonight. He went around the room and had everyone try to find something to be thankful for. Listening to everyone was very humbling. I sat there with Cathy's words laying heavy on my heart. She could be right; it might be time to try looking for a studio apartment. I help clean everything up and set up for the morning. When I get to the kitchen, I find Pastor Clarence waiting for me.

"Have a seat, Mick." He's not even touching the cookies; now I'm worried.

"Cathy told me what she said to you earlier."

"Is that why your sermon was different tonight?"

"Yes. She had no right to judge you or anyone, for that matter. You're staying here is not putting anyone else out. You've been a big help to me and I wouldn't change a thing."

"Then why do I hear an underlying but?"

"There will come a point when you will need to take that next step. I just want to let you know that I will understand when that time comes. You have made so much progress in such a short time. I don't want you to ever doubt that

128

progress."

"Thank you, but you need to make me a promise that if you need me to leave, just tell me. I won't be offended."

"You've got a deal. Now, what about those cookies."

His hearty laugh is a comfort. I pour the milk and pass him the cookies. "I've been thinking about looking for an apartment. The problem is, I need a job. My disability payments won't cover everything, and I'm not sure what type of job I should even look for."

"Well, you're good with your hands. What about construction? Or security? There are always openings. We have a job coach that comes in here on Wednesday. His name is Dusty Monroe. You should sit down with him and see what might be available to you."

"That works out great; I have counseling on Tuesday and Thursday this week."

"Well, I better back away from these cookies and get some sleep. Thanks again for helping organize all the coats. We are doing another round of distribution this weekend."

"I'll make sure I'm there to help. Goodnight, sir."

He leaves and I clean up and head to bed. Since I've been seeing Dr. Finley, the nightmares have been better. As I drift off I keep reminding myself that I'm a work in progress.

The days are getting shorter and colder. When I get to the bench, I see Raven across the street with Jax. I'm about to leave when she sees me and darts across the street. "Sorry I'm late today." She passes me a bag and a coffee.

"Thank you."

"Mick, walk with me to school."

While we walk to school, she's telling me all about her adventures with Jax. It sounds like she's decided to give him a chance.

"Mick, tell me what I can do to help you move forward in life?" It's hard for me to make her understand how much her just being here and listening to me has changed my life. She takes my hand and squeezes it. "Mick, let's sit for a bit; I'm early."

We sit down and I immediately notice all the added security around the playground. "Raven, why are there more guards?"

"Wow, nothing gets past you. Jax informed me that there have been some threats to Michael and he wanted to make sure he is safe. It's just a precaution; don't worry."

After a few minutes of silence, "You—just being here and listening to me—is all the help I can handle right now." I glance around and commit to memory how many guards there are. I will keep an eye on the school grounds, too . . .just to make sure."

"Mick, you're a wonderful guy and, someday, you'll realize it. I have to go in; the bell is going to ring. Have a great day."

After making sure she gets inside, I head to my appointment with Dr. Finley. I have a good feeling that things are finally coming together for me.

Chapter Nineteen

I get Dr. Finley's office and Stacey, the nurse, informs me he's been called out on an emergency. Today's appointment has been bumped to Friday. She informs me that he left a note for me.

"Stacey, can you read it, please?"

"Mick, I have an experiment for you. I would like you to walk down into a subway station. You don't have to get on the train; I just want you to take that first step. Be brave, and I'll see you on Thursday."

Jesus, he can't be serious. I head outside and even though there is a crispness in the air, I feel the sweat bead up on the back of my neck. I start walking up the avenue, stopping at every entrance. Unable to go down. I pull out his note and read it again, like I'm expecting to see something different. Maybe if I stand on the grates, I can work up the nerve to go down the steps. I'm waiting, but no train. The only thing this is accomplishing is pissing off the people that have to go around me. The more I stand here, the more ridiculous I feel. I walk over to the steps and begin my descent into the bowels of the city. Okay, not really the bowels of the city but it sure feels like it. When I get to the bottom, there are turnstiles and a booth. I lean up against the wall toward the booth, trying not to look to conspicuous. Suddenly, I hear the train pulling into the station. I close my eyes and try not to lose it. The smell of the metal-on-metal brakes is a twisting knot in my stomach. As the train stops, the noise gets louder. My eyes are still closed and in my mind I'm replaying the last moments of the plane crash like a viewfinder. I'm yelling at Dom "Eject, eject, now God damn it, now!"

I feel someone grab my arm. Usually I would reach out in self-defense but not today. I open my eyes and a transit cop is asking me questions.

"I'm sorry, I missed what you were asking me."

"I said, are you okay?"

"Yes, I'm doing my homework assignment," I tell him. He cocks his head to the side and raises his eyebrows in disbelief. "My shrink gave me an exercise to do. I'll be leaving now." Before he can answer I head back up the steps to civilization. It might be a baby step, but for me that was a huge leap of faith. I walk the rest of the way back to the mission. I think I might have a little bit more spring in my step. When I get to the mission, I notice there is a man standing outside. The same man that was with Jax this morning.

Before I can say anything, he thrusts his hand out toward me. "Hi, Mick, I don't know if Raven mentioned me;

I'm Maxwell Fleming. I'm in charge of security for Jax and his company, Raiders Inc."

"Actually, no. What can I do for you?"

"It's more like what can I do for you? I understand a little bit about your situation and I was wondering if there is anything I can do to help you?"

Why the hell wound this guy want to help me? "Thank you. I'm sorry you went out of your way today, but I'm fine." I'm sure he has the best intentions but I really don't need a handout. "If you really want to help, we could always use another set of hands." I don't give him a chance to say no. I open the door and he follows me inside.

"So, Mick, tell me about this place."

"It's different from other places I've volunteered at. They have all kinds of programs to help from job training to drug counseling. Would you like a quick tour?"

"Yes, please."

He is quiet as I give him a tour of the place. When we get to the thrift store, he raises his eyebrows and seems amazed when I tell him I built it all in less than a week. "The details in the woodwork are amazing. You did all of this dovetail work?"

"Yes, I enjoy getting lost in the work."

"Have you thought of doing this for a living?"

"No, I'm not sure what I want to do, yet. It's almost time for dinner. I need to get on the line. We could always use an extra set of hands if you're interested."

"Lead the way, mate."

We head to the kitchen and get everything set up. He rolls up his sleeves and gets right to work. The lines today are longer than usual, but they don't seem to faze Max at all. When the last person is through, we begin to break everything down and he starts washing the pots.

"Thank you, Max."

He stops and turns to me. "For what?"

"I'm sure you weren't expecting to spend your day helping out here, let alone washing pots."

"Mick, I've never had a problem getting my hands dirty. We all walk a different path in life. I don't judge anyone without all the facts."

"After clean up, Pastor Clarence holds a sermon. If you're interested, you're more than welcome to join us."

"Thanks, but I need to get going. Remember what I said, if there is anything I can do for you, please don't hesitate to ask."

He leaves and I'm not sure what to make of the man. He seems to genuinely care, but he also seems troubled. I'll talk to Raven tomorrow about him.

I get to Starbucks, but no sign of Raven. When I check the time, I realize I must have missed her. I was expecting to get here early but it seems with the weather getting colder, the mission is getting busier. I'll go by the school later. The weather is so beautiful, I decide to walk for a while. No clue where I'm going or even where I want to be. When I step into the corner store for a bottle of water, I notice a sign to buy a Metro Card. I take a deep breath and hand the cashier twenty dollars for a card and a bottle of water. He also gives me a New York City Subway map. I must look like I need it. I think I want to try the subway again. Who knows, maybe I will find the courage to actually get on the damn train. I head across the street and go down the long flight of steps. All the while, mentally reminding myself I'm in New York City not Iraq and not on a plane. Thank God, it's not rush hour and the station is practically empty. As I swipe my new metro card, my heart begins to pound. What the hell was I thinking? I close my eyes and try to steady my pounding heart. I can hear the train coming as I open my eyes and begin to back away.

"For Christ sake, Mick, grow a set and get on the train!"

The train begins to slow down and the screeching of the brakes makes the sweat bead on the back of my neck. When two doors finally open and I'm still standing there, I realize I might just be okay. I take a step forward and the doors immediately close behind me. Well, hell, I guess there is no backing out now. I grab the pole and watch as the train pulls out of the station. There is only one person in the car. He's playing around on his phone, not paying any attention to me. I take a seat next to the door, so I can easily jump out if I want to. The stops are short, but I pull out my journal and make some notes. I find I'm getting used to the breaking noise and, before long, I find ways to tune it out. I'm so proud of my success; I can't wait to share it with Raven. I pull out the map and figure out what train will get me to Raven's school. I know I'll be early but maybe I can catch her at recess. Besides, lately, things seem a little off at the school.

When my stop finally comes, I head out and take the steps two at a time. I don't know why, but I have a feeling I just need to hurry up and get there. I race up to the school as the kids are lining up to go inside. Suddenly, two men with guns jump out of a van and charge toward Raven! Another set of men have Max and they are beating him pretty bad right before they inject him with something. I'm racing toward Raven when I get grabbed from behind. Two of the men begin hitting me. I'm trying hard to fight them off. One man hits me on the side of my head with the butt of his gun. When I drop to the ground they start kicking me. Raven is screaming. I'm trying to get up so I can help her but I can't. I feel the blood running down my face. The last thing I see is one of the gunman hit Raven before tossing her and one of the kids in the back of the van.

Chapter Twenty

I wake up in the emergency room and Max comes running in. He looks pretty beat up but it doesn't seem to have slowed him down. "Max, did you find them?"

"No, why where you there? Did you know anything about this?"

I feel a rage inside of me I never felt before. I try to take a swing at him but he catches my hand in midair.

"I didn't think so, but I had to ask. Why where you there?"

"I had a breakthrough today and I wanted to share it with her. I know I was early, but I thought I could catch her at recess. Something was telling me to get to the school. Lately, when I'm at the school things just feel a little off. Do you know who has her? Do you know why they took her?"

"No, I don't know who has her, but they also took Jax's nephew, Michael. I don't know why they were taken, but I need to get to Raiders. I know they all had masks on but do you remember anything about the van?"

"I remember part of the license plate—three, nine, three—it was a blue panel van. There was no lettering on it. It was there the other day, which I thought was strange. I thought maybe it was maintenance people."

"That's great, Mick, if you remember anything, please let me know right away. I'm leaving some security in place here, just in case."

"Please keep me posted." It's more of a plea than anything else but it's all I've got. He runs out. The nurse comes in and informs me the doctor wants a CAT scan since my head was cracked open.

"Is all this really necessary? I need to get out of here."

"I don't know what you're thinking but you are not going anywhere." She helps me into the wheelchair and we head out with security not far behind us.

When we're finally done, I'm back in my room with a severe headache. Apparently, the doctor wants to keep me in the hospital. I still haven't heard anything from Max. This is ridiculous. I'm not sitting around here, doing nothing. I need to find my clothes and get the hell out of here. I'm about to get up when the door swings open and Jackie walks in. She looks so pale and young.

"Jackie, is there any news?"

"No, but I brought you some coffee." Her hands are trembling as she passes me a Starbucks cup.

"Thank you. Hopefully, this will help my headache. Can you stay for a bit?"

"Yes, as long as you don't mind another security guard?

I promised Max I wouldn't ditch him."

She sits in the chair next to the bed. She seems off. "Jackie, what is it?"

"I was supposed to be on that playground not Raven. We switched at the last minute."

"You can't blame yourself. I don't think it would matter who was out there. They had a plan and no one was stopping them. Hell, both Max and I are proof of that."

"Are you going to be okay staying here? I mean I know you don't do well in confined spaces. Not that Raven told me all your personal stuff, but she had me cover for her when you needed to go to your appointment and stuff. Jesus, now I'm rambling on and making no sense at all."

I take her hand and squeeze it a little. "It's okay. I told Raven she could explain to you about me. I'll be okay here, but I much rather be out there trying to find her. Do you know why anyone would want to kidnap them?"

"Probably money. Greed will make people do desperate things."

The nurse comes in and informs us that I need to get my rest. Apprehensively, Jackie leaves but not before she programs her number into my phone. I close my eyes and keep replaying the events of the day over and over again, trying to remember anything that might help. It all happened so fast. "Why, God, why are you putting *so much* on me?" I don't know why I expect him to answer me.

I pull out my journal and read my notes from today. I'm lost in the words, when I hear the door open. I look up and see a beautiful woman staring at me.

"Hi, can I help you?"

"Hello, my name is Anwan. I didn't want to bother you, I just wanted to thank you for trying to rescue my grandson and his teacher today."

"I only wish I could have done more. Do you know if they heard anything yet?"

"No, I'm headed to Jaxson's office now. I just wanted to thank you. I'm sure Maxwell will keep you updated." She squeezes my shoulder, turns and leaves.

I look at the time and decide to call Pastor Clarence before I close my eyes for a while. Before I can call him, there is a knock on the door and he steps in, clutching a bag.

"How did you know?"

"Your friend that helped out yesterday called me to let me know what was going on. What can I do to help you?"

"Get me out of here so I can help find Raven."

He pulls a chair closer to the bed and takes a seat.

"That's not going to happen. You need to heal."

"What's in the bag?"

"Cookies."

"They are limiting my visitors; how did you get in here?"

"I told them I was your pastor and you needed me."

"I do. Why? Can you tell me why God thinks I can carry the weight of the world on my shoulders? I'm just a simple guy, trying to make it through life."

"He never gives us more than we can carry. I know you don't like that answer but it's the truth. You're a strong man, yet, you keep wanting to give up . . . doubt yourself."

"I can't survive another loss. Everyone around me dies."

"This life we live here is temporary, at best. All we can

do is try to be the best person we can be, and then hope for the best."

"That's it? That's all you got?"

"Well, that and cookies."

He gets up and shakes my hand. "I promise I will keep her in my prayers. Let me know if you need anything. I better get out of here before I wear out my welcome."

He leaves and I pull out my journal but I can't concentrate on anything. "God, if you can hear me, please bring them home safe. I know I keep asking you for help but she is so much to so many—please."

I close my eyes and keep my phone clutched tightly in my hand. I don't want to miss anything, but my head is pounding. I must have drifted off because when I open my eyes, the sun is filtering through the blinds. I look at my phone; there is a text message from Max.

Max: They are safe. I'm sure Miss Raven will want to talk to you in the morning.

"Thank you, Lord."

There's a knock on the door and the nurse comes in.

"Good news; you're being released today. The doctor should be in shortly. Is there anything you need me to do for you?"

"No, thank you." She leaves and I take a quick shower. The doctor walks in just as I finish up.

He goes over the confusion protocol and he reminds me that I need to follow up with my regular doctor about my stitches. I don't care about any of that; all I know is, I want to see, for myself, that Raven is okay. The nurse comes in with the wheelchair and she gets me downstairs. We are about to exit when, the doors open and Raven is standing there. I literately feel all the air leave my lungs. I can't get out of the damn chair fast enough. She heads to me and gives me a big hug. I look at Jax and he's smiling. The few times I've met him, he's never really smiled.

"Mick, thank you for trying to help us. I'm so sorry they hurt you." She's giving me the once over, just like a mama bear making sure I'm okay. We head over to a bank of chairs and take a seat.

"Raven, I'm sorry I didn't get to the school sooner to stop them."

She's sitting next to me, rubbing my arm, offering comfort. "Why where you at the school?"

I look down at the floor and then back at her. "The other day, when we walked to the school, I noticed the van. It felt off to me. So, I thought I would keep a closer eye on you. Like I said, I'm just sorry I didn't get there sooner." I want to tell her about my breakthrough but that's too personal to share in front of everyone.

Jax steps up and extends his hand. "I'm grateful that you tried to help my girl and my nephew. I would like to help you, and before you say anything, please listen to me."

He holds his other hand up to emphasize his point. "We could use a man with your proven courage. You stepped up to the plate to help, when nothing was expected of you. A lesser man would have turned away. Just promise me you'll think about it."

He reaches into his back pocket and pulls out a business

card wallet. He retrieves one of them and passes it to me.

"Here is my card; when you're ready, call Max or me. And, again, thank you."

He extends his hand and again I shake it. "Thank you."

"In a few days, let's get together so I can tell you everything that went on and I want to know everything that's been going on with you."

We get up, I give her a hug and watch her leave. When she is finally out of sight, I feel a wave of emotion come over me. I take stock of all that I have and put aside all that I have lost. I know there is no going back. There are no do-overs in life. The only thing we do have is one shot at a second chance. It took me a while to realize it, but I got mine. I'm going to hang on to it as tight as I can and never let it slip though my hands again.

Epilogue

It was on a New York City bench that my life changed forever. They say in life you can never go back. Yet, for a brief moment in time, I was able to. Whether it was just my mind playing tricks on me or it was my minds way of trying to heal. I have no clue. What I do know is that giving back to others literally put me in the path of a woman who would change my life forever. We bonded over the horrors in our lives but instead of them making us cynical or cold-hearted. We chose to give back. With her support, I learned I'm not damaged goods.

Little did I know, the woman who came into my hospital room, to thank me that day, would become my everything. Anwan showed me that love knows no boundaries. Tomorrow is not promised. She taught me I could love again and not feel guilty about it. There will always be a special place in my heart for Shay, but there is plenty of room for Anwan and our entire family . . . a family by choice.

The End

Other Books

The Unraveled Trilogy

The Unraveling of Raven

Darkness Into Dawn

Shattered Lies

Uniquely Mine

The Letter: Dear Michael

About the Author

Theresa Sederholt was born and raised in Brooklyn New York. She is a graduate of Campbell University in North Carolina, with a degree in Criminal Justice. Theresa now calls North Carolina home, with her husband, a professional chef, and her two dogs.

Experiencing life first hand is what she does best. Believing she can do anything has put her in many crazy situations. Whether it's babysitting a pig farm or cutting the top off of a mini truck; nothing is ever out of reach. Her list is endless, A to Z.

Theresa's beliefs are pretty simple. There isn't a luggage rack on the hearse, and give a girl Nutella and espresso and she can change the world.

Theresa enjoys connecting with her fans. She can always be reached through her website at:

www.theresasederholt.com

www.ingramcontent.com/pod-product-compliance
Lightning Source LLC
Chambersburg PA
CBHW060431130626

46555CB00005B/2312